OTHER MINDS
and Other Stories

BENNETT SIMS

Two Dollar Radio
Books too loud to ignore

Two Dollar Radio
Books too loud to Ignore

WHO WE ARE TWO DOLLAR RADIO is a family-run outfit dedicated to reaffirming the cultural and artistic spirit of the publishing industry. We aim to do this by presenting bold works of literary merit, each book, individually and collectively, providing a sonic progression that we believe to be too loud to ignore.

TwoDollarRadio.com

Proudly based in
Columbus
OHIO

@TwoDollarRadio

@TwoDollarRadio

/TwoDollarRadio

Love the
PLANET?
So do we.

Printed on Rolland Enviro.
This paper contains 100% post-consumer fiber, is manufactured using renewable energy - Biogas and processed chlorine free.

100%   **PCF**   BIO GAS   PERMANENT

Printed in Canada

SOME RECOMMENDED LOCATIONS FOR READING:
In a theater waiting for a movie to start, at the food court in the mall, on a bench in Villa Borghese, or pretty much anywhere because books are portable and the perfect technology!

AUTHOR PHOTO→
Carmen Maria Machado

COVER DESIGN→
Eric Obenauf

Two Dollar Radio would like to acknowledge that the land where we live and work is the contemporary territory of multiple Indigenous Nations.

Versions of these stories appeared in the following publications: 'La "mummia di Grottarossa"' in *The Iowa Review*; 'Unknown' in *The Kenyon Review*, as well as in the Pushcart Prize Anthology; 'Pecking Order' in *Ploughshares*; 'Portonaccio Sarcophagus' in *The Georgia Review*; 'Afterlives' in *Tiny Nightmares*; 'Minds of Winter,' 'Introduction to the Reading of Hegel,' and 'A Nightmare' in *Conjunctions*; 'The Postcard' in *Socrates on the Beach*; 'Medusa' in *BOMB*.

For Liz

CONTENTS

OTHER MINDS
and Other Stories

LA 'MUMMIA DI GROTTAROSSA'

IN THE BASEMENT OF THE PALAZZO MASSIMO museum in Rome, there is a vault called The Strong Box. Beyond the numismatic collection and the vitrines of golden jewelry, in the middle of the rearmost room, a display case exhibits the blackened body of a mummified Roman girl. She was embalmed in the second century AD and left undiscovered until 1964. She lies in a glass box, her arms at her sides. Today, living children crowd around this coffin, taking photos with their phones. Compared with her, the hundred statues on the floors above them bore them. Old white stone, marble that was never mortal. They ignore the inorganic Aphrodites, Antinouses, Medusas. They can tell that this girl, despite the two millennia condensed in her, is closer to them in time. Like them, she once lived inside it. Now she has passed beyond it. She can teach them things the statues cannot. Her dark body is like the negative of their bodies. Seen from the side, the mummy is as stiff and straight as a minus sign: that hyphen that haunts all negatives, all knowledges lying beyond the zero on the number line. At the entrance to The Strong Box, on the threshold of the -2nd floor of the museum, the wall text that is her epitaph promises many treasures: *The numismatic collection. The historical medals. The ancient jewelry,* it reads. *And other preciousness.*

UNKNOWN

AT THE MALL A WOMAN ASKED TO USE HIS PHONE.
Excuse me, he heard from behind. He had just bought A's birthday gift, a new phone from the AT&T store. He was passing through the gauntlet of kiosks on his way to the mall's exit, and he assumed that one of the stalls' sales clerks was calling out to him, inviting him to sample cologne. He ignored the voice and kept walking. But the voice followed after. Excuse me, sir. Sir. Please, sir.

When he turned there was a small older woman holding up a heavy purse in both hands. She thanked him and made eye contact. Trapped, he waited for her to ask for money. May I borrow your phone, she asked instead. I need to make a call. It's an emergency. He hesitated. If it was an emergency, why was she asking a stranger, rather than a security guard, or the clerk at the AT&T store? He felt certain it was a scam. But when he revolved the scenario in his mind, he couldn't make out what the nature of the scam would be. The worst she could do, it seemed, was take the phone and run, or fling it to the ground.

Please, she said. It's important. I was supposed to call five minutes ago, and I'm already late. It's an emergency, she repeated, and she gestured vaguely in the direction of the AT&T store, where a young boy and girl were peering through the shop window. Neither turned to look back, and it wasn't clear whether they were with her, or whether the emergency concerned them. He considered lying, claiming that his battery had died, but something in her gaze seemed to anticipate the lie, and he felt this path blocked by guilt. It's no trouble, he told her. He took out his phone and tapped the passcode into the lock screen. He swiped open his settings and disabled Bluetooth, then opened his email and logged out. He handed her the phone. Oh, thank you, sir. She held it in one hand while she dug through her purse with the other. From the bottom of her bag she withdrew a second phone—a newer model, the same model, in fact, that he had just bought for A, not at all an inexpensive phone—and began tapping at it deftly. He felt instant alarm. He still didn't understand the scam, or where the danger might lie, but he did not like the sight of this woman's phone. Wait, he told her. Why don't you make the call on your own phone? She was glancing from her screen to his, typing something. Without stopping or looking up she answered: I have no data. I need to find the number. All the politeness and gratitude had drained out of her voice. When she had finished typing, she smiled and stepped aside, holding his phone to her ear. He told himself to remain calm. There were hundreds of witnesses around them. It wasn't as if she could run away with his phone. And even if she did, what did it matter? It was only a phone. He could go back to the store and buy a new phone.

While waiting for her friend or whoever to answer, she hunched over, hugging her purse to her chest, in the posture of someone cramped into a phone booth. He maintained enough space between them to respect her privacy, but he was still close enough to eavesdrop, and when at last she spoke, he pretended to scan the crowd while straining to listen. He could only pick out snatches. She was whispering angrily. You'll never find me, he thought he heard her say. Never. Her tone—though low—was vehement. She continued in this vein, her voice rarely rising above a murmur. Whoever was on the other end of the line must have been listening in complete silence, for there were no pauses in her monologue. She seemed to be gloating. I escaped, he thought he heard her say, or, It's too late. You'll just have to find someone else, he thought he heard her say. Finally she hung up and handed him his phone. Thank you so much, sir, she said. You are my savior. Thank you.

She walked off in the direction of the food court. He turned to the shop window, but the children were no longer there. Perhaps they were waiting in the food court to meet her, or maybe they had already left with their real mother. He opened the phone to check the recent calls. There were none. The last number dialed was A's, from earlier that day. Either the woman had deleted her call from the list—was this possible?—or she had not called anyone at all. Had simply delivered her monologue to a dead phone. When he glanced back at the food court, the woman was gone. He couldn't find her anywhere in the crowd.

Back home, while preparing her birthday dinner, he told A about the woman. He recited what he could remember of her monologue. When he'd finished she asked who he thought the woman could have been talking to. It sounds like a stalker, A said, a jealous lover. Maybe she didn't want to call from her own phone because she was used to being tracked. Or maybe, he suggested, it was a debt collector. Or a probation officer. In any case, A said, a happy story. With a happy ending. She got away.

After dinner he gave A her presents: the phone, and tickets to a play that weekend. They sat on the couch together, and she transferred the SIM card from her old phone to the new one. He helped her link the device to his Find My Phone program, in case she ever lost it, and while she set up her other applications he took out his own phone. The object seemed compromised in his hand. He couldn't rid himself of the suspicion that the woman had done something to it. It felt changed, charmed. He opened its browser and searched *Lending strangers your phone*. He skimmed an article and read the most alarming passages aloud to A. In one scam, he read, a stranger will ask to use your phone and pretend to dial a number or text their friend. In reality they'll be opening your payment applications and transferring funds to themselves. You don't have any payment applications, do you? she asked. He shook his head. I won't install any either, she said. In another scam, he continued, the stranger will call their own phone to harvest your number for identity theft. Sometimes they'll even call a criminal enterprise—a drug dealer, for instance—so that your number will be on file in their records: later they'll try to use this information to blackmail you. Somehow I don't think that's what she was doing, she said. No, he agreed, it didn't sound like she was talking to a drug dealer. Why not just take her at her word? she asked. He nodded. But when he tried to imagine who the woman could have been talking to, no one came to mind. What had made A so certain it was a lover? He imagined himself on the other end of the line, listening quietly to that monologue. How he would never find her. How he would have to find someone else. How she had escaped.

Later that night, while they were reading in bed, A's new phone kept vibrating on the nightstand. She would reach for it, tap at its screen, set it aside. A minute later it would vibrate again with a new text message. Now she had placed her book down and was holding the phone in her hand, as if to muffle the buzzing with her flesh. When it vibrated again she swiped it open and tapped a short reply. Out of the corner of his eye he could see the blue and gray bubbles of a text thread, but he couldn't make out the name of the contact or what she was typing. Her expression betrayed nothing. She set her phone back down on the nightstand. What's the news, he asked, without looking up from his book. No news, she said. Birthday wishes. She did not say who from, and he resisted the urge to ask. He was gripped by the image of a strange man, a handsome man, on the other end of the phone: alone at a restaurant table somewhere, sending messages to her. He didn't know where the thought had come from. Whenever she texted in bed—never very often—she usually told him who it was, and it was usually one of the women she worked with. That was probably who it was now. There was no man. The woman in the mall—all this talk of stalkers and lovers—must have put the idea into his head. He was jealous of a phantom. He tried to focus on his book, but her phone vibrated again, buzzing against the hard wood of the nightstand, and the sound of it sawed through his concentration. He willed himself to ignore it, his chest tightening at every noise. She tapped at the screen. He still couldn't see the contact name, could just make out gray bubbles popping into view, surfacing from an unknown source. With each new bubble the phone buzzed in her palm. Can you maybe put it on silent, he asked. She touched his shoulder and kissed his forehead. I'm sorry. She silenced the phone and placed it in her nightstand drawer.

At the same moment his own phone vibrated on the nightstand beside him. Unknown, the screen read. He declined the call. Who was it, she asked. It's an Unknown, he said. He had learned to ignore unlisted numbers. If it were a real person, they would leave a voice message. It was almost never a real person, just a computer text-to-speech program. The recordings followed a similar script: he was notified that he had committed some oversight or crime—he had defaulted on a debt, there was a warrant out for his arrest—and he was given a number to call back at once. This is an emergency, the thin urgent robotic voice would insist. The scam was structured like an anxiety dream. The voice of authority enveloping you, with its spotlight of guilt, to remind you of something you should never have forgotten: the final exam you hadn't studied for; the meeting you were already late to. And then the way you simply accept whatever identity the nightmare assigns you, like an actor possessed by a role. He imagined that some people must respond to these robocalls as he did to his anxiety dreams: the credulity, the panic, the waves of shame. The scam must work part of the time— people must actually call the number and divulge their personal information—or else the calls would stop.

I thought you had blocked unlisted numbers, she reminded him. He regarded the phone with puzzlement. She was right. Now he could remember: about a month ago he had begun receiving several Unknown calls a day, and he had called AT&T for help. They had looked up his account and blocked unlisted numbers for him. He hadn't received any Unknown calls since, not until tonight. That's right, he told her, I did. So how did an unlisted number get through? He thought he heard suspicion in her voice. He opened the phone and checked the recent calls. The Unknown usually had a strange area code, from a state he had never visited. If he searched the number online, he could find message boards full of other people who had also received calls from it, offering each other advice, warning each other not to answer. But when he checked the missed calls log now, there was no number. It just read Unknown. The caller had not left a voice message either. His first thought was of the woman in the mall. Who had she dialed today? If they were determined to find her, they might call him back. They might even be determined enough to mask their number, to circumvent blocking software.

I don't know, he answered finally, they must have some kind of… program. Just put it on silent, she suggested. He switched his phone to Do Not Disturb and put it away. She took her phone from the drawer and continued tapping at its screen. He reached for his book, pretending to read.

It wasn't until his lunch break the next day that he remembered to deactivate Do Not Disturb. When he did, his screen cascaded with alerts for missed calls and new voice messages. Most were for work, one from A. But one was another missed call from Unknown, no number listed, and this time they had left a voice message. It was half a minute long. Normally he would delete it without listening, but today he pressed Play and pressed the phone to his ear. He heard A's voice. It sounds like a stalker, he heard her say, a jealous lover. Or maybe, he heard himself say, it was a debt collector. Or a probation officer. In any case, he heard her say, a happy story. With a happy ending. She got away.

He played the recording back. Their voices were distant and echoey, and it was clear what had happened: his phone's microphone must have recorded their conversation during dinner last night. His phone had been lying on the kitchen counter, where it would have been able to pick up both their voices. He supposed it was possible that there had been a malfunction: the microphone could have turned on spontaneously, and the resulting recording could have been mistakenly saved to his voicemail. It didn't seem likely. But the other explanations seemed even less likely, and more disturbing. Because what if the woman at the mall were responsible? What if, while pretending to talk, she had actually downloaded spyware onto his phone, some kind of eavesdropping program? Maybe she could remotely access his microphone now to listen in on him, and maybe she had sent him this recording as a threat, in advance of future blackmail. Or maybe it was not the woman who was responsible, but whoever she'd been talking to. She had called them from his number, after all, and now this person—whoever they were— might be training their powers of detection and surveillance on his phone, instead of hers. They could have hijacked his phone in their quest to find her and ended up finding him. Wasn't that what she had said to them? You'll just have to find someone else? She could have passed them on to him, the way you pass on a curse, setting into motion a chain of displacements. Now the Unknown would just substitute his phone in her place, calling again and again until he called back from someone else's number.

He pictured a debt collector. He pictured a probation officer. But the more he listened to the recording, the more likely it seemed that A had been right. This was something that a stalker, a jealous lover, might do. When the woman had called them from his phone, and his unfamiliar number had flashed across their screen, he could imagine their reaction. First the confusion, and then—when they heard her voice—the rage. So, they would think, he thought, this must be her new lover's number. Such a person would likely go on calling that number indefinitely. Hacking the microphone. Leaving menacing messages. The moment he handed the woman his phone, he realized, it had become entangled in her story. It was no longer his private property, just a prop in this other drama. Far from stealing his identity from his phone, she had contaminated it with her own.

He played the recording back. A happy story, he heard A say. With a happy ending. She got away. If the recording had been made by the woman's stalker, the message it was meant to send would be clear. She may think she has gotten away, but they were still listening.

He opened his phone's browser and searched *Microphone remote listening*. He searched *Microphone malfunction*. He spent the rest of his lunch break reading about security breaches.

That night he played the recording for A. Creepy, she said. He deleted it. He told her about an article he had read at lunch. Apparently there was a bug in their phones' conference call feature: if someone dialed your number, then quickly added their own number to the conference call, your microphone would activate while your phone was still ringing. Then the caller could listen in for as long as it took you to answer or to decline the call. The article warned readers to check their phones: if they had any mysterious missed calls, someone might have already exploited the bug. That must have been what happened, he told her. That Unknown call. Who would do that, she asked. Anyone could do it, he said. He watched over her as she disabled the conference call feature on her phone.

But later that night, while they were reading in bed, a detail began to trouble him. The recording in his voicemail had been made at dinner. That was when they had discussed the woman in the mall. Yet the Unknown caller had not called until later, when they were already in bed. He picked up his phone. A's phone vibrated on the nightstand, and he ignored it. He checked his calls list and confirmed it: there had been no missed calls during dinner. Her phone vibrated again, and she tapped her passcode into the screen. According to the article, the eavesdropper could listen in only while the phone was ringing. So last night, there would have been only a ten-second window in which the Unknown caller could have recorded them. They had been in bed when the call had come. But they had been in the kitchen when the recording was made. A's phone vibrated in her hand while she was still typing her response, and she paused a moment to read. Whoever made the recording, it followed, could not have been exploiting the conference-call bug. They would have had to listen in through some other method, which meant that disabling conference calls would do nothing to prevent them from listening in again. They could be listening in right now. Now he regretted deleting the voice message. He wished he could listen to it one more time, or play it for someone at AT&T.

A tapped at her screen. What's the news, he asked her, and in his ears his voice already sounded disembodied, mechanical, as if he were overhearing a recording of himself. When he looked over at her phone he could see the blue and gray bubbles of a text thread, but she pressed the lock button and the screen went dark. No news, she said. Something at work. She's lying, he thought, and the thought alarmed him. The thought seemed to come from somewhere outside him. She set her phone to silent and put it aside. He opened his own phone's browser and searched *Recovering deleted voice messages*.

At work the next day he installed a file organizer for his phone on his laptop. The program could organize the contents of your phone's hard drive into easily searchable folders. If there was still a copy of the recording anywhere on his phone—even in a deleted folder or in its unallocated space—the program would display it. Then, if he did find it, he could use the program to recover the file.

He plugged his phone into his laptop. All its folders were immediately visible in the program's sidebar: voicemail, photos, recordings, texts. He tapped his phone's screen, and it prompted him to enter his passcode. The device was still locked, internally. But the program must have circumvented the lock on his laptop. He clicked on the *Texts* folder. The threads were arranged in a list, organized by contact, with his most recent contact—A—at the top. He clicked her name. Their entire correspondence was visible: her messages to him, his responses, each time-stamped to the second. He scrolled up several screens, moving back months in their relationship. The silly fights, the accusations, the reconciliations. All of it was open to him. He had not needed to enter his passcode to read them. He had needed only to plug in his phone.

And if his phone didn't need to be unlocked, he realized, then neither would hers. All he would have to do was plug it into his laptop and open the program.

He scrolled through the file organizer and clicked on *Voicemail*. He clicked on *Voice memos*. He clicked on *Deleted files*. He could not find the recording anywhere.

When he got home from work, A had laid out dresses on the bed. He asked whether she had dinner plans, careful to keep the suspicion out of his voice. A smirked and reminded him that the play was tonight. He had forgotten all about the birthday tickets. Do you need to shower too? she asked, and he shook his head. I won't be long, she told him.

While they were getting ready, he kept an eye on her phone. He had his laptop out on the bed and prepared: the program open, his phone plugged in with a USB cable. It would take only a second to unplug his phone and substitute hers in its place. He didn't even need to read the texts themselves. All he wanted was to see who had been messaging her. He would check the contact's name, verify that it was one of the women she worked with, and unplug her phone. But she didn't leave her phone unattended. Even when she took her shower, she brought it into the bathroom with her. Through the bedroom wall he could hear the muffled voice of a broadcaster echoing off the bathroom tiles. She never listened to the news when she showered. She was doing it tonight, he found himself thinking, only to keep her phone away from him.

He looked at the laptop in bed, trailing the white spy siphon of its USB cable, and felt ridiculous. What was he doing? If she caught him reading her texts, he didn't know what she would do. He had never done anything like this. A week ago it would never have occurred to him. It was the kind of thing that the Unknown caller—the woman's stalker—might do. He had allowed this hypothetical jealous lover's jealousy to infect him. He had become possessed by someone else's possessiveness, paranoia, obsession.

The shower cut off and A silenced the news broadcast. When she came back into the bedroom, clad in a towel, she set her phone on the nightstand. From the bed he watched her get dressed. Eventually she went back to the bathroom to put on makeup, and this time she did not bring her phone with her. She left the bathroom door open. He heard water running in the sink. He didn't have much time. He unplugged his phone and connected the USB cable to hers. It buzzed once against the nightstand, and he held his breath at the noise. But the water kept running in the sink. In the program her phone appeared as a paired device, and he clicked the *Texts* folder in the sidebar. Without bothering to skim the list of threads he clicked the topmost conversation, her most recent contact. The contact had no name. She had saved their number under Unknown.

The cunning of this stunned him. This way, he realized, the contact could text or call her even when she was at home: there would be no danger of him glancing over at her phone's screen and seeing their name, since it would just read Unknown. He scrolled up the thread. There was no mistaking it. The messages were all timestamped. Unknown was the same person she had been texting in bed the past two nights, the same person who had been sending her so-called birthday wishes and updates from work. He skimmed the most recent messages hurriedly, trying to absorb as much as he could before she returned. There was a string of gray bubbles in a row, no blue bubbles in response. *You'll never find me,* he read. *You'll just have to find someone else.*

The sink fell silent and he heard her opening the mirror cabinet. He X-ed out of the program and unplugged her phone, stuffing the USB cable into his nightstand drawer and slamming his laptop closed. When she came into the bedroom he was lying fully dressed in bed. She paused in the doorway, regarding him. Are you ready? she asked. Yes, he said, I just need to use the bathroom. He thought his voice had been neutral, but she asked, Is everything all right? He kissed her forehead on his way to the bathroom. He locked the door behind him. He ran water in the sink and sat on the toilet.

He went over the messages in his mind. She must have been texting Unknown—whoever they were—about the woman in the mall. She must have been quoting the woman's monologue. But if that were the case, the text bubbles would have been blue. He tried to visualize the thread. *You'll never find me. You'll just have to find someone else.* He felt sure that all the bubbles had been gray. Which meant that Unknown had been the one to text them to her. Which meant that she must have already told this person about the woman beforehand. She had shared this story—his story—and now it must have become something of a running joke between them. *I'll meet you at the mall tomorrow,* she would text them. *You'll never find me,* they would text back, *you'll just have to find someone else.*

He was jumping to conclusions. Maybe Unknown was not a code name at all: maybe it really was an Unknown caller. She could have received these texts from an unlisted number, perhaps even the same unlisted number that had been calling him. The woman in the mall could have easily obtained A's information. While she had been tapping at his phone's screen, pretending to dial, it would have been trivial for her to open his contacts list and copy the numbers. Now she could be texting A the same monologue he had overheard her reciting into his phone at the mall. And if not the woman herself, it could always be her stalker who was sending the messages. If they could hijack his microphone, make remote recordings, they could also hack his contacts and send messages to A.

But if she had been receiving strange texts from an unlisted number, why not tell him?

She knocked on the bathroom door. We're going to be late, she said. I'm coming. I'm finished. He bent over the sink, splashing enough water on his face and hair that she would register the wetness, then turned off the faucet. When he opened the door she had her phone in hand, as if to check the time.

A t the theater they silenced their phones. As they walked down the hallway he noticed—alongside the No Smoking signs and Emergency Exit maps on the walls—newer signs forbidding electronic devices. In the illustration, a monolithic black slab was centered in a red circle, with a barred line running through it. To be safe he took his phone from his pocket and turned it off altogether, holding the power button until it had finished shutting down.

Inside the theater they found their seats in a middle row. They hadn't talked much on the ride over, and they did not talk now. She'd asked once in the car whether something was wrong, and he had said that nothing was wrong—he was just tired. But he wasn't tired. He had never felt more awake. Tomorrow he would get to the bottom of it, he had decided. While she was asleep, he would take her phone and his laptop into the bathroom. He would use the file organizer to download Unknown's texts, saving them all to his laptop as a PDF, and then he would be able to read them at his leisure. He held her hand as he planned this. She read the playbill. He pretended to scan the crowd.

As people settled into their seats, they opened their phones to silence them. Screens glowed to life in the rows around them, then fell dark. The theater lights stayed on while the crowd accomplished this. It was as if the play were waiting for a perfect seal to form between itself and the outside world before it started: as if the curtains would not part until the last phone had been silenced, until there was no portal remaining through which reality could irrupt into the theater, disturbing the play with a foreign logic. When the lights finally dimmed, the audience grew quiet. Everyone turned toward the stage. But just as it seemed that the curtains were about to part, a cell phone rang out from the back row, cutting through the stillness.

It was a shrill, insistent marimba—the same ringtone, in fact, as A's—and it reverberated throughout the theater. Something about the acoustics of the space must have amplified the noise, for it sounded impossibly loud, less like a ringing phone than a fire alarm, as if it were being blared from the theater's speakers. He could feel the vibrations in his chest. He shifted in his seat, resisting the urge to crane his head toward the back rows, as the people in front of him were already doing. Their glares, he knew, would magnify the guilt of the phone's owner. At the sight of this sea of turning heads the culprit would dig even more anxiously through their purse, their pants pocket, frantic to find the device and shut it up or off.

But they did not shut it off. It went on ringing, far louder than an average phone and for far longer than it would take the average person to locate their phone, far longer, even, than it would take for the average phone to default to voicemail. Maybe it was buried at the bottom of a heavy purse, impossible to find, or maybe the phone's owner had gone to the bathroom and left it behind as a placeholder on their seat. He pictured a glowing screen, lying face up on the cushion, reading Unknown. He pictured a panicked finger stabbing at the screen, missing the red decline button every time. The crowd began to murmur, and he felt a mob hostility rising against the phone and its owner. Who forgets to silence their phone? How could you ignore all the signs in the hallway? And even if you had, how could you watch everyone in the seats around you silencing their own phones without remembering yours? What call could be so important— what news could you be expecting—that you wouldn't just set the phone to vibrate? At least it was ringing now, he thought, before the curtains had parted, and not midway through a monologue. But still the play would be delayed. It would not start until this final phone had fallen silent.

From the back of the theater, the phone kept ringing. Turn it off, he thought. Turn off your phone. As if she had overheard this thought, A bent to her purse and withdrew her phone, double-checking that it was silenced. On her screen he glimpsed what looked like an alert for a new text, then she put the phone away. Someone behind him muttered, Turn it *off*, and in the row ahead a man took out his phone to examine it. The crowd was getting restless now. He turned around, searching the back rows, but he couldn't find a likely culprit. No one was standing and patting their pockets. People were turning to each other in their seats and shrugging. The phone kept ringing. Exasperated, he took out his own phone. He knew he had turned it off already, but he was gripped by a compulsion to check.

He pushed the home button. To his surprise, the screen glowed to life. The phone must have been on this entire time. If he hadn't thought to check, and the Unknown had called him in the middle of the play, *he* would have been the disruption, the locus of the audience's loathing. But that was impossible. He had a clear memory of turning off his phone when they arrived. Could it have turned back on in his pocket? Maybe he had been sitting on it at an odd angle, putting pressure on the power button with his thigh. Or maybe, he thought, the Unknown had turned it on remotely. Could they do that? In principle, he supposed, it was possible: if they could activate his microphone, they could turn on his phone. He held the power button and watched it shut down a second time. He placed it on the seat cushion, the glassy black screen face up, so that he would see if it turned on again.

At the same moment the phone in the back row fell silent. Everyone returned their attention to the stage, and the crowd began to murmur good-humoredly. All the tension in the room relaxed. At first he did not understand. Then a prerecorded voice delivered a message through the theater's speaker system: Don't be that person, the voice intoned. Please remember to silence your phone.

Now he understood. The ringtone had been a recording. The rude theatergoer was a fiction, a decoy designed to attract the hatred of the crowd. The theater had played the ringtone in the same way that ornithologists will play back birdcall recordings in the woods: just as a flock will sometimes mob a trilling amplifier, trying to drive away the phantom intruder, the crowd had turned on this nonexistent audience member. Just as there was no bird in the speaker, there was no phone in the back row. It was a virtual point, an empty center toward which real vectors converged. And it had worked: everyone had double-checked their phones. No one wanted to occupy the place of the decoy themselves. No one wanted to be the person who received a call during the play, to have the crowd turn on them. The theater would replay the recording for the next audience, and the next, and with each iteration this illusion—ghostly, acousmatic, a call haunting them from an unknown source—would set off the same chain reaction in the crowd. Everyone's behavior would be bent by this nonexistence.

He reached for A's hand. The curtains parted, and the play began.

During his lunch break the next day, he tested the file organizer with his phone. He opened the *Texts* folder and selected A from his contacts, clicking the *Export as PDF* button. It took longer than he expected—almost five minutes—but in the end their entire correspondence was saved to his desktop. The interface could not have been simpler. It would just be a matter of getting hold of A's phone.

He reached to unplug his phone, but he stopped when he noticed the Voicemail folder in the program's sidebar. There was one new message there, according to the file organizer. Strange, he thought, that he had somehow missed it on the phone itself. He felt sure there hadn't been an alert. Unplugging the phone, he checked the missed calls now and saw that, indeed, he had one new message: another voicemail from Unknown, a minute long this time. He pressed Play and pressed the phone to his ear. He heard A's voice, or a woman with a remarkably similar voice. I think he's been reading my texts, he thought he heard her say. There was a long silence, as if she were waiting for someone to respond, or as if the response had not been recorded. I'll meet you tomorrow, he thought he heard her say. The same place. She hung up and the recording ended.

He checked the timestamp. He had apparently missed the call and received the voice message last night, when they had still been at the play. So the woman on the recording could not be A. She had been beside him in the theater the entire time. She'd left him only once, during intermission, to use the bathroom. Was he supposed to believe that she had made this call from the stall? That the Unknown had hijacked the microphone on her phone too?

He listened to the recording again, with earphones this time. He maxed out the volume. He strained to distinguish background noises—flushing toilets, sink faucets, hand dryers—but heard nothing other than A's voice, or a voice remarkably similar to her voice. It could not be A's voice. Even if the Unknown had hijacked her microphone—even if they had happened to record her half of a phone call last night—there was no reason for them to send the recording to him.

The likeliest explanation was that this was a wrong number. Some other woman had tried to dial some other lover and had reached his phone instead. It sounded like A only because he was primed to believe it was her. The recording confirmed what he wanted to hear, confirmed his worst fears, so he heard A's voice in it. When in fact the message could be from anyone. There were lots of unfaithful partners in the world, lots of jealous lovers.

On the other hand, if A really were meeting someone somewhere today, it would be trivial to check. He opened his Find My Phone application and logged into her account. The map loaded, searching for her phone's GPS location. If he was right, and this voice message were the result of a wrong number, she would be at work as usual. The map zoomed in on the mall, and he saw a blue dot pulsing in the gray wasteland of its parking lot. So. She was at the mall. But that didn't mean she was meeting anyone there. She could have brought her phone to the AT&T store, to complain about the strange texts she'd been receiving. He watched the blue dot for a minute, but it didn't move from the parking lot. Maybe she was sitting in her car. Or maybe she had left her phone in the car while she went inside.

He called. It took five rings for her to answer. I'm at work, she said. What's up? He said he'd misdialed and apologized for bothering her: he would see her at home.

He called into work and said that he wouldn't be returning from lunch. He drove toward the mall, leaving the map open on his phone. As he sped down the highway, he kept glancing over to the screen. Her blue dot didn't move. Every time he checked, it was pulsing in the same place in the parking lot. Then, halfway to the mall, the dot disappeared. It evaporated off the map, as if it had never been there. She must have turned off her phone, or switched it to airplane mode.

When he arrived in the parking lot, he circled the vicinity where the blue dot had been, but he couldn't find her car. His phone vibrated, and the screen read Unknown. He declined the call. He switched his phone to Do Not Disturb and entered the mall.

He walked up and down the main hallway, searching the crowd for her face. Excuse me, he heard from behind. A woman's voice. Excuse me, sir. He turned and saw a sales clerk at one of the kiosks, inviting him to sample cologne. He ignored her and kept walking. At the AT&T store he paused to look in through the shop window. A woman with two children was at the counter, talking to the clerk. She seemed to be returning a phone: she handed a white box with a receipt to the clerk, who scanned its barcode with his laser.

He moved on to the food court. At the tables there were mostly families, groups of teenagers. But at one table he saw a handsome middle-aged man sitting by himself, with no food. He had placed his phone on the table before him and was tapping at the screen. Discreetly, he moved past the man and sat at a table a few rows behind him. The whole time he watched him, the man never looked up from his phone, not until he pocketed it and rose to leave. Careful to maintain a safe distance, he followed the man. He trailed him across the food court and out the mall's exit. In the parking lot, where A's car was still nowhere to be seen, he watched the man climb into his own car and drive away.

He returned to the mall. He brought his phone to the AT&T store and explained about the Unknown caller. The clerk looked up his account. That's strange, the clerk said. Unlisted numbers weren't blocked anymore. Maybe when he had bought the new phone, the clerk suggested, it had reset his account somehow, restoring the default settings. The clerk called AT&T's customer service, and they reactivated the block.

He returned to the food court and sat by himself at the same table. He deactivated Do Not Disturb, expecting a missed call or text from A. But the only alert was for a new voice message from Unknown. The timestamp was from earlier that day, the call he'd declined in the parking lot. He pressed Play and pressed the phone to his ear. I know you're lying, he heard himself say. The voice on the recording was strained and angry, and he had no memory of saying the things it was saying. But still, it really did sound like his own voice. Or it sounded unlike his voice in the same disembodied, mechanical way that all recordings sounded unlike him. He recoiled to hear it. *Tell* me, he heard himself say.

The message cut off. He played it back. The more he listened to the recording, the more it sounded like himself. Except he knew he had never said these things. It had to be a recording of Unknown. But whether this message was meant for him, or for A, or for the woman in the mall, he could not tell. In the end, he supposed, it did not matter: it was the last message they would be leaving, now that the block was reactivated. He deleted it.

He opened the Find My Phone map and refreshed it, waiting for A's blue dot to rematerialize. When the time came that he would normally return home from work, he pocketed his phone and left.

B ack home, the house was empty. A's car was gone, and— when he checked the closet to confirm—her suitcase.

He sat at the dining room table, waiting for the call. The longer he stared at his phone, the more his confusion turned to rage. He imagined A somewhere with a strange man, a handsome man. He kept picturing the man he had seen in the food court, though he told himself that this was irrational. He tried calling her, but her phone went straight to voicemail. He hung up before the recording started and pushed the phone across the table.

Five minutes later the phone rang, displaying an unfamiliar number. When he answered, he heard A's voice, or a woman with a remarkably similar voice. She was speaking low, and it was hard to hear over the sound of the crowd around her. He could tell from the background noise and the echo that she was in a public place, spacious with high ceilings. He didn't know what number she was calling from—whose phone she had borrowed—but he supposed it might be possible for him to track it. He did not speak, only listened quietly to what she had to tell him. She was whispering angrily. You'll never find me, he thought he heard her say. Never.

I escaped, he thought he heard her say, or maybe, It's too late. You'll just have to find someone else.

OTHER MINDS

THE READER WAS READING AN E-BOOK IN A CAFÉ. Whenever he arrived at a sentence that other readers had highlighted, a pop-up notification would display how many times it had been underlined. The reader had come to dread this feature. No matter what genre of novel he was reading, the same type of sentence was always underlined: maxims about love. If a sentence began *Love was...* or *Being in love meant...*, it was sure to have a dotted line running underneath, with the notification *650 other readers have highlighted this passage.* Meanwhile the rest of the novel would remain unmarked. Pages of precise description, dinner-party set pieces, digressions—the kind of language that he would have underlined with his own pen, if he were reading a physical copy—would go ignored, as though they had made no impression on these other readers at all. Today's novel was no exception. He clicked ahead, skimming the highlighted passages: *The secret of love...*; *That was what being in love was.* Apparently the only language that other readers loved, the reader was coming to realize, was language about love. He could not understand this. He could not imagine what was going on inside these other readers' minds, while they read. Whenever he came across a precise description—of someone's thoughts, of a field, of a dinner party—a little pleasure would light up in his brain, yet when these other readers came across that same language, he supposed, their brains must remain blank, their minds as inert and slate-gray as the e-reader's screen. The boredom *he* felt when reading maxims about love must be what *they* felt when reading about thoughts. The pleasure *he* felt when encountering a sentence with a thought tag in it (*he thought*; *I imagined*; *it dawned on her*) must be what *they* felt when encountering copular propositions about love (*Love was...*; *Being in love is...*). It was hard to fathom, but the evidence of the highlights was undeniable. In the beginning, when he had first bought the e-reader, he had felt superior to these other readers. More sophisticated. They must lack the taste, he told himself, or the judgment, to appreciate the sentences that he did. Or else, he found himself thinking, they must have highlighted their own sentences mindlessly, at the prompting of the pop-up, for no other reason than that the passage had already been highlighted by so many previous readers: as though each reader were like a walker following the same shortcut through a field, he imagined, flattening it further and contributing to the desire line that would go on calling to future walkers. He no longer felt this way about the highlights. By now he had read enough e-books, and encountered enough underlinings, that he had begun to suspect that his mind was the one that was missing something. Tens of thousands of readers had been moved by these maxims about love—so moved that they had placed their fingertips or their styluses to the touch screens of their devices and had physically caressed the sentences—and these same tens of thousands of readers had meanwhile passed over precise descriptions of thoughts and landscapes with perfect indifference, numb to their pleasures. What the e-reader had revealed to the reader was just how far he was outnumbered by this numbness. To these other readers, he knew, his mind would be the curiosity. Why did he care more about landscapes than love? What was wrong with him? All his life, if someone had asked him why he read, the reader would have answered that he was curious about *other minds*. He read to learn how other minds saw, thought, experienced the world. He believed that his own mind could be reflected and enlarged by the language of other minds. Even if he found a book boring, it was enough to remind himself that another mind had produced this boredom—that another brain perceived the world in this boring way—to revive his interest and inspire him to finish. But ever since discovering the highlight feature, he was not so sure he wanted to learn any more about other minds. Increasingly the thought of other minds disquieted him. When six hundred readers highlighted a sentence about love, or ignored a precise description, that certainly gave him an insight into their minds. But it was not an insight that he desired, if anything he felt isolated inside it, locked in a loneliness indistinguishable from solipsism. The idea that he was the only reader in the world underlining precise descriptions frightened him. It would be like attending a dinner party, he imagined, where you were the only guest to order dessert, and where you noticed all your friends wincing one by one as you brought a spoonful of ice cream to your mouth, and where gradually it dawned on you that for these people—perhaps people you had known for years, whose inner lives and sensory experience you had always taken it for granted resembled your own—for them ice cream must taste like ash, and where finally, to seal your dread, you would watch on in horror as each of them delicately dipped their spoons into the tables' cigarette trays and fed on actual ash, sucking from their spoons like hummingbirds at a feeder, to savor the flavor. You might not want to stay at such a dinner party very long. You might not want to learn how else their minds diverged from yours, indeed you might even begin to suspect—not just that they possessed other minds, different minds—but that they did not possess minds (or what you would recognize as a mind) at all. Robot minds, yes, possibly pod-person minds, but not human minds. The reader set his e-reader down and looked up at the café, studying the faces of the other people around him. Many were silently reading their own books, magazines, tablets, phones. Even now, he thought, were they underlining maxims about love? Some of them could be the very same readers who had left highlights in this novel. Some of them could be highlighting the novel right now. Their minds were a mystery to him, and more and more that mystery was beginning to seem menacing, and mutual. He packed his e-reader and gathered his things. He would stop by the bookstore on the way home, he decided, and buy a physical copy of the novel. As he crossed the café, some of the other readers glanced up from their devices and smiled at him, and he wondered for the first time what being read by them might be like. How would these other readers read him? If he were to precisely describe his own thoughts, he thought—if he were to write about his experience as a reader, about how it felt to encounter *other minds*, and if he were to post it on the e-book store for others to read—would any of these readers recognize themselves in his descriptions? Would they find something in them, in him, worth highlighting? Or would they skim his thoughts with impatience, waiting for what his mind had to tell them about love? He left the café and headed in the direction of the bookstore. His mind would be boring to them, he knew. They might force themselves to read on, even to finish, but there would be nothing there to underline. He did not think his thoughts had much to do with love. Unless, it dawned on him, as he arrived at the bookstore, this was also what love was. He stood outside the entrance, thinking. Unless the secret of love just was this boredom, he thought. A little pleasure lit up in his brain. Excited, he continued past the store and hurried home. Back at his apartment he went straight to his computer and began to type. He would write it down, he decided, and he would see. He would post it on the e-book store and see. Because what if that was what being in love was after all? Learning to look into an other's mind, even when it was mind-numbing? Even if you would not highlight a single line it was love.

PECKING ORDER

IT FELL TO KYLE TO KILL THE CHICKENS. ON Saturday before dawn, while Audrey was still asleep, he put on an old T-shirt and jeans and headed out to the coop in the backyard, hedge clippers in hand. It was a cloudless cool morning, and though the horizon was still dark, the hens were already up and clucking: all three were making the warbling underwater sound that meant he was late letting them out. The coop was a shed-like wooden trailer with mesh windows along the sides and a hatch-style door in back, where a two-by-four gangplank dropped down to the ground for the hens to file in and out on. Theirs was the only coop in the neighborhood. The yards to either side were furnished with barbecue grills and birdfeeders, and he scanned the porches for any sign of the neighbors, sipping coffee at their banisters. The yards were empty, the windows dark. No witnesses.

The chickens had been Kyle's idea. He and Audrey had rented the house after college and had treated it as a laboratory for locavorousness. They kept a garden in the backyard. They could walk to the farmer's market. When they absolutely needed to go to the grocery store they biked to the Trader Joe's in black track suits at midnight before garbage day, gleaning the dumpster out back for plastic clamshell containers of wilted salad mix, expired Odwalla juice, and six-pack cartons of cracked or otherwise compromised eggs. Back home they tested the eggs by dropping them one after the other into a pot of cool water: half usually buoyed to the surface like witches, and of the unrotten ones on

the bottom, one or two would discharge venereal-looking drib-
lets of white albumen from invisible fissures in their shells. One
weekend, after every egg in the batch bobbed rottenly, he started
browsing Craigslist for coops. He and Audrey had never owned
a pet together, but he was eventually able to talk her into the
idea, on the condition that he assume full responsibility for the
chickens. And for the past few years, with the help of YouTube
tutorials and farm FAQs, he had. He woke early to feed them
and biked home at lunch to check in. He taught himself to rac-
coon-proof the coop. Soon he and Audrey had enough eggs
in the fridge to cook frittatas every weekend, and they hadn't
paid a single dollar to the region's overcrowded, groundwater-
polluting poultry farms.

But sometime this past winter their little micro-flock—almost
simultaneously, as a group—had quit laying. And although
Audrey had cajoled him into keeping them for a while, as pets,
there was no point putting it off any longer. Last month he had
been accepted to law school, and at the end of summer they
would be heading east. Since they couldn't bring the chickens
along with them, the time had come to slaughter them. Audrey
knew of a good butcher at the farmer's market, but it felt cow-
ardly paying a stranger to do what he could do just as well himself, here in the backyard, where at least the chickens would feel
at home. The YouTube how-tos made it look straightforward.
He searched the garage the other day and found the hedge clippers in a corner. Technically they belonged to the landlord, but
he planned to bleach them afterward.

When he showed the clippers to Audrey that night she
frowned and ran an appraising finger along the blades. Weren't
they too rusty, she asked? Too dull? If he was going to do it

himself she didn't want it to be painful and inhumane, she said. He did not ask her—who had done nothing to help care for the chickens—when she had become such an expert in butchering them. He just nodded thoughtfully. What did she suggest? She went to the kitchen and dug their toolbox out of the pantry, handing him their wood-handled hammer. Not a sledgehammer, or a mallet, just the dainty claw-headed thing he'd destroyed his thumb with hanging up picture frames the weekend they moved in. It looked about as deadly as a plexor. She didn't appear to be joking. In defending the clippers he proceeded to mock the hammer maybe too meanly, calling it their poultry Mjölnir, destroyer of coops, and asking her how many painless, humane hammer blows she thought it would take to knock a squirming hen unconscious. By the time they went to bed he thought he'd sold her on the clippers.

But the next morning, while they were both at work, she texted him links to butchering tutorials on YouTube. The same videos, naturally, he'd already looked up himself. He skimmed through them again on mute, to humor her: three-minute clips of rosy-cheeked men in overalls cheerfully demonstrating different instruments of death, which ranged from industrial-grade, machine-whetted cleavers and hatchets to, yes, mallets. But the most impressive of the videos displayed what seemed to be a motorized garroting gadget: a noose of steel wire protruding from a white plastic housing, which—with the push of a button and an evil, mosquito-like whine—would begin to reel the wire in, cinching it tighter and tighter around a chicken's throat until, inexorably, within seconds, the head would pop free on a parabola of pressurized blood. As he skipped around in the video that morning, it occurred to him that all that the high-tech device was doing was basically what a pair of hedge clippers would. It was the same principle, in the end: incremental constriction, scissors physics. If they could clip hedges they could clip heads. He said as much to Audrey when he got home. As long as I don't have to see it, she told him.

Holding the clippers now, paused on the plank of the coop, he was trembling with what he recognized from high school football to be adrenaline. He had never killed an animal before. He had never even been in a fistfight. Was it legal, actually, to be slaughtering livestock in a residential backyard in plain sight? He'd been afraid to google it. What if the neighbors saw? What if the neighbors' children did? What if they called the police, or PETA, or Audrey? He gave the clippers two quick neutering snips in the air. They were the heavy-duty pruning kind, with long bowed handles capped in green plastic and with two curved blades that clamped together in a tight metallic beak. They would probably be fine. Everything would be fine. He just needed to squeeze fast and hard on the handles, apply enough crushing pressure to their necks. It would take seconds. He would be back in bed before daybreak, and later this afternoon he and Audrey would be defeathering the carcasses and roasting them for the big goodbye potluck they had invited everybody over for tomorrow. Normally they would never serve meat, but it would be a way of honoring the chickens, they agreed, to share them with friends: to make of them a meal that had been raised and loved locally and killed with compassion by the very same hands that cooked them. It had seemed then—and still did seem this morning—like the most dignified death he could offer the animals.

Leaning the clippers against the coop, he stepped into the dim interior, where he was assaulted by a wall of straw odors.

The chickens were huddled together on the roosting shelf, their small sharp funnel faces all regarding him with their left eyes—the far-sighted, predator-seeking eye—as he approached. He petted each in turn before scooping up Simone. He told himself that he had picked her first at random, but the truth was that he was expecting her to be the easiest, emotionally, to murder. She was—alone among their flock, if not among her race—an appalling bully and greedy sociopath. Within the first month in the backyard she had managed to grow twice as fat as the other two chickens by aggressively gobbling down their share of feed, and in the time since she had enforced her primacy in the pecking order with psychotic ruthlessness, jabbing Hannah and Judith with her beak, clawing at their eyes, ripping the tail-feathers brutally out of their bottoms, sometimes without even the provocation or the pretext of food to compete over, just for the sake of humiliating them, which sadistic displays of dominance he had often watched with rage from the kitchen window. He had read that feather-pecking might be stereotyped foraging behavior, and that providing stressed or anxious hens some litter to peck at was supposed to help. But he had added litter to the yard, and if anything this had only made Simone torment Hannah and Judith more, jealously driving them away whenever she noticed *them* pecking at it. It was no use complaining about any of this to Audrey, who doted on Simone and sometimes let her ride her shoulder like a parrot. She's just a chicken, she chided him. You can't get mad at her. This after the incident last year, when he'd caught Simone mounting Hannah in the yard and snapping at her eyes. The only way he could think to get Simone off her was to make an empty fist around some phantom feed and go *tss tss tss* while jerking it, as if calling her to peck pumpkin seeds from his palm. Food was the only bait more tempting to that little hobgoblin than blood, and sure enough she dismounted Hannah to waddle hungrily over to him. When she was within kicking distance he punted her back toward the coop. The betrayed yelp she made—it was a sound he had never heard a chicken emit before or since—had the same mewling, pseudo-human quality that kicked dogs are capable of. Audrey, who had been watching this for God knows how long from the kitchen doorway, shouted his name across the yard as sharply and shamingly as if the chicken had been their child. Just a chicken, she had said to him then, and he had never understood what she meant. Parrots could count. Crows could not only remember human faces but bear grudges against them. Who could say what Simone was thinking? If a chicken could think, it could hate, and be hated. If Simone could think, he *could* get mad at her. But if she could think, and feel pain, he also couldn't kick her, he knew. He had apologized, and told Audrey she was right, and given Simone one of Audrey's hair ties, one of her favorite toys. But even though he had only ever lost his temper like that the one time, both of them—Audrey and Simone—had kept a cool distance from him for days afterward.

Now, though, as he held Simone in the crook of his arm, she seemed at peace with him. She let out soft *bgawk*s, scrabbling gently at his forearm with her talons as he carried her down the plank and grabbed the clippers with his free hand. He had taken her out of the coop hundreds of times on days just like this one, and if she had detected his apprehension—if she intuited (by the sight of the hedge clippers, or the firmness of his grip) that today was going to be any different—she did not try to flee. She trusted him. Holding her tight, he crouched down in a bare patch of dirt and positioned her between his knees, squeezing them together to pinion her wings. At this she did seem nervous, growing still with fear, and he effortfully effleuraged her comb to calm her. Then he collared her neck with the hedge clippers, no doubt sparking some species memory of a fox's jaws. She blinked rapidly and cocked her head at acute, confused angles, the way she always did when encountering a strange or novel object, weaving around it in the grass to investigate: she was trying to see her death, too, with each eye. He squeezed the handles.

The blades glided deeply through the meat at first. Sooner than he had expected he heard the homerun crack of what he assumed was a vertebra being snapped, but then the blades got caught on something and locked up. Simone spasmed between his legs, thrashing her head, and he had to wrestle with the hedge clippers like a steering wheel to steady her. A jet of blood spurted wet warmth across his forearms, shirt, and face, and, wincing, he pressed his knees together, waiting for Simone to fall limp. He listened to the drawn-out sound of her *bgawk*s, which soon elongated into deafeningly shrill, ear-splitting screams. They sounded to him almost like human screams, like the unmistakable scream of the murdered at their murderer, which must sound the same, he thought, no matter what creature is screaming it. It was as if this death rattle could adapt itself to the anatomy of its victim, emerging as a single sound from any throat, such that when murdering a chicken you'd hear the same curse against you as when murdering a person. At this thought it occurred to him that Simone's banshee *bgawk*ing was liable to wake Audrey, or the neighbors, and he scanned the surrounding windows. All still dark. Simone's throat's blood—which had spurted upward at first—appeared to be losing pressure. It cascaded down in a single sheet, darkening the feathers of her belly and muddying the dust at his feet. The blood loss alone was enough to kill her eventually.

But she did not stop spasming or screaming, and now the other two chickens had started shrieking alongside her from the coop. Hannah and Judith had pressed their faces against the mesh window, and as they watched their sister's execution they beat their wings and bawled in unison, driven to a state of choric frenzy by the gore. The sound of their voices must be what was encouraging Simone, for she kept kicking her legs in a futile attempt to flee, as if trying to run back to them. Her talons clawed the ground, scarifying the dirt with a series of scared parallel lines. This was impossible, he thought. She could not still be alive. He counted to ten out loud, as though disciplining a child (*If you're not dead by the time I get to ten...*), and when Simone continued to struggle he understood that she was not going to die, not if she hadn't already. Not only had he failed to decapitate her, he had failed to even sever a vital artery. His breaths became tight, and it was as if it were his own throat between the blades: as if his future—this necklace of inevitability and dread—were constricting around him now. He had no idea what he was doing. That much was becoming clear. What if Simone refused to die? Even if her head came off she might find a way to live, like that one sideshow chicken who'd survived eighteen months beyond its decapitation, thanks to a protruding snorkel of spinal cord that had preserved its brain stem. Simone, too, could lead a half-dead headless heedless life like this: Audrey would insist that he care for her, pipetting corn kernels into her neck stump with an eyedropper, and Simone would no doubt hang on indefinitely, haunting him like a Dullahan.

He tried squeezing the hedge clippers' handles again, to drive the blades in deeper, but almost immediately he met a gristly resistance. The blades were being blocked by an obdurate bedrock of muscle and bone. He waggled the handles in panic, clenching them until his fingers ached, and he felt the same frustration and rage as he had in kindergarten arts-and-crafts, whenever the dull blades of the hateful safety scissors would get stuck in some uncuttably thick piece of construction paper. He felt like throwing a tantrum, like flinging the clippers from him. He relaxed his grip and breathed. There was no use losing his temper. He needed to kill Simone as quickly and as painlessly as possible.

His mind raced through all the myriad ways of killing Simone. He imagined stomping on Simone and stabbing Simone. He imagined punching Simone and kicking Simone. He imagined prying up one of the garden's flagstones and using it to bash Simone. Above all else, he needed to put Simone out of her misery, and it didn't matter how he did it, just so long as he did it soon. Every second that he wasted was another second of unspeakable suffering for Simone. Every second that he kept these blades buried in Simone was another second of barbaric torture for Simone, far worse than anything she would have had to endure at a factory farm, where at least death was mechanized and mass-produced, designed to minimize fear, pain, and discomfort, with the hens likely locked into metallic leg restraints and dangled upside down from a shackle line, whose motorized belt would convey each of them to a water stunning bath to dunk them under, one after the other, submerging their heads for the precise time it takes an electric shock to knock a squirming hen unconscious, before raising the limp oblivious birds and gliding them toward the private compartment at the end, through the flap of black plastic that blocked their view and baffled sound, beyond which a pair of pneumatic scissors would—with a hiss of air—snip their throats above the spill trough. Even Simone deserved a death like that.

He pulled apart the handles until the blades unstuck and threw the clippers to the ground. Blood poured freely from her neck, where the opened wounds made two thin dark slits in her skin like gills. Dizzied by the sight of the blood, he reached down with both hands and grabbed her head, wrenching it as far as he could to the right. He had only ever seen spies or assassins snap necks in movies, and they always made it seem as clean as this. You gave the head one orthopedic, orthogonal twist to the side, and there was the sudden foley effect of crunched ice. Except this did not happen with Simone. When her head hit the outer limit of cervical rotation it simply stopped, grinding to a halt, and she made some kind of awful drowned burbling sound, still fighting to breathe through the fluids filling her throat. His hands were slippery and syrup-colored with the blood that was choking her. He could barely feel anything through the sopping feathers. He knew he needed to hyperextend her head by another few inches if he wanted to kill her, but the more forcefully he tried to torque her spine, the more nightmarish her burbles of pain became. Her squawks were now arrhythmic and hiccupy and horrifying to hear. This only made him more impatient to snap her neck, so he started swiveling her head back and forth, jerking it left and right in energetic bursts. It felt like jiggling the knob of a locked door: as if he were trying to open the door to her death, only to find it locked with life, deadbolted against death by the unrelenting cylinder of her life. With every jerk he felt the dumb stubbornness of her skeleton, the brute anatomical fact that a neck doesn't *want* to be snapped. What was wrong with him? Why couldn't he snap this neck? It was only a chicken's neck. He had snapped curtain rods and kindling thicker than this neck.

The harder Simone resisted, the more he began to resent her. Why wasn't she cooperating? Didn't she understand he was doing her a favor? She was fighting death with the same viciousness with which she had bullied Hannah and Judith. Yes, of course, that was it exactly. The gluttonous little shit was as greedy for life as she was for feed, and now she was bullying Death out of his fair share, competing with him over every last grain of sustaining oxygen. She was trying to establish a pecking order over Death! Even a chicken understood that death was inevitable, that it was preferable to die quickly rather than to prolong the agony, but Simone was prolonging the agony anyway. She was probably drawing out the agony just to spite him, ruining her body for consumption. He thought with bitterness of all the cortisol and adrenaline that were doubtless even now flooding out of her brain and into her bloodstream, tainting the meat with the taste of her terror. With every second that she didn't die, more and more mortal horror was leaching out of the cortex and into the meat, she was only growing more acrid with each protracted nociceptive second that passed. The flesh of her breast was becoming a kind of telltale heart against him, contaminated with that telltale tartness, and he could already picture Audrey at the potluck tomorrow, screwing up her face in disgust and discreetly spitting out sour white wads of Simone into her napkin.

Simone managed to get a wing free from between his knees and began flapping it, as if waving to Judith and Hannah for help, and this somehow made her neck even stiffer and harder to twist. He released one hand to wipe the slippery blood off on his jeans, and she took advantage of his loosened grip to dart her beak blindly at him, biting into the web of skin between his thumb and forefinger. He hissed at the sting and flapped his hand, shaking the pain out of his purlicue, and to keep Simone from fleeing he squeezed his knees even tighter against her sides, so tight he thought he felt a rib breaking. Good. Let her rib break. Let all her ribs break. She wanted to fight dirty, fighting death? She wanted to enforce a pecking order? He would show her how high up on the pecking order he fell. He was a primate! A linebacker! He used to bench three hundred pounds! He hunched over her, clasping his hands around her skull. Without allowing himself to think, he yanked up on her neck with all his strength, in a single whole-body motion, as if trying to clean-and-jerk a feathered kettle bell. As he rose, her neck stretched elastically with him, but he kept her torso pinned below, between his knees. He felt more than heard the silence that resulted. All at once the air became dewy with quietness, which was the sound—it took him a moment to realize—of Simone *not* screaming. She had stopped burbling and *bgawk*ing and clawing at the dirt, and this was how he knew, as he kept rising, that her head was about to tear loose from her body. Her head tore loose from her body.

There was a wet ripping sound, the word *ligaments* flashed into consciousness, and then there was no more resistance to be felt. He was yanking with all his strength on nothing, on absence and air, and the upward momentum sent him staggering backward. He steadied himself just in time to see Simone's decapitated torso topple over, her throat's stump pumping dark blood into the dirt with little systolic burps, like a discarded garden hose. He averted his eyes, glancing down at his hand, but what he saw there was even worse: his fingers were still clutching—had forgotten to drop—Simone's head. Her beak hung open in a soundless shriek, like some muted Orpheus, and her left eye was staring right, sightlessly, at him. Without thinking he flung the head away from him, and it bounced across the grass like a skipped stone before rolling to a stop beneath the coop. There it landed looking up at Hannah and Judith, who started squawking in hysteria. They are in Hell, he thought. They must think that they have woken up in Hell. He glanced down at the hedge clippers, which indeed looked demonic in the aftermath: the heavy blades were greased with blood, brown feathers and flecks of bone spattered across them. And he wasn't even done with them. He was only one-third finished. At this thought all the strength drained out of him. Judging by the milky light boiling over on the horizon he had only an hour or so before the neighbors woke, and in that time he needed to take care of both Hannah and Judith, then hose off whatever extra blood and brains their respective death throes would have succeeded in spraying across the yard. He needed a break before he could face it. A glass of water.

Turning to the house, he saw Audrey at the kitchen window, pale and stricken. Christ. He lifted his shirt above his stomach to rag away the blood on his cheeks as he approached the back porch. She was standing in the doorway when he got there.

'Babe,' she said. 'That was awful.' He couldn't tell by her tone whether she was accusing or commiserating.

'I cut at the wrong angle,' he explained. He shook his head in self-reproach, and even as he did so he recognized the gesture from other goof-ups, other mechanical misjudgments, like the time he had tried to fix the chain on her mountain bike or assemble their sofa. I threaded the chain wrong, he had said then, shaking his head, or: I screwed this rod in backward. He had just cut at the wrong angle. It's not like he had relished ripping Simone's head from her body. One day this would all be funny.

'I told you those hedge clippers were too dull,' Audrey said. 'What you need is that hammer.' And she went inside the kitchen and headed for the pantry. He followed after her, glancing down too late to confirm that his bloody boots were tracking Simone across the linoleum. He'd mop up before the potluck.

'There's nothing wrong with the clippers,' he said. He could overhear the petulance in his voice. But it was absurd to blame the clippers. If they could cut through a branch they could cut through a chicken spine. Except that a branch doesn't struggle or fight back. Or scream. 'I just need to cut higher up on the neck,' he said.

Audrey still had the same pale stricken look on her face, and it was as if she were seeing him five minutes in the future, ripping Hannah's head from her body. No. Even if the hedge clippers did get stuck again, he wouldn't have to fight with Hannah or Judith, not as he had with Simone. She had long since pecked a submissiveness into them, had disciplined them in advance, and they would know to go docilely into death. They would file into its depths as obediently as they were used to waddling down the coop's back plank, especially after what they had just witnessed. Still, to placate Audrey, he joined her in the pantry and rooted through the toolbox.

He held up the hammer. 'Worse comes to worst,' he told her, popping the air before her face. She flinched.

'Do you want me to help this time?' she asked.

He shook his head, and she did not bother concealing her relief. She went back to the window, where he knew she would be watching. 'It will be fine,' he said. And he believed it. If the hedge clippers failed to decapitate the chickens cleanly, all he would have to do is take the hammer in hand and, as mechanically as if he were cracking crab shells, deliver one or two taps to their skulls. Swift. Painless. Humane. They wouldn't even have time to scream. And if the hammer didn't work? On his way out the door Audrey touched his shoulder, he assumed to encourage him. But when he leaned in and kissed her cheek, she reflexively raised her fingers to the spot, as if brushing away a lipstick imprint of blood.

THE NEW VIOLENCE

THE FELLOWSHIP WAS IN ROME. SHORTLY AFTER arriving, the writer planned to screen an Italian horror film in his studio. It was set in Rome in the 1970s, a classic of the *giallo* genre, in which a killer in black leather gloves murders multiple victims with a meat cleaver. The writer invited all the other fellows to attend. Some were artists like him, but most were scholars. Whereas he was there to write fiction, they were there to write monographs, and every week they shared their research with each other. On the day of his screening, it turned out, an archaeologist had offered to lead a tour of a nearby museum. Its pottery collection, numbering hundreds of black-figure jugs, included the subject of her monograph, a famous Etruscan jug dating back to the seventh century BC, and she invited other fellows to accompany her. After lunch that day a large group set out down the hill from the Academy. The writer decided to go as well. For several hours the archaeologist led them past glass cases of fat orange amphorae, across whose curved surfaces the dark silhouettes of mortals and gods impaled each other with spears or bit into each other's brains. Eventually their group arrived at the Etruscan jug, isolated from the others on a pedestal in a small showroom. The jug was celebrated for its scrolling portrayal of a battle scene, in which conquering soldiers stab their enemies. As she led them around the pedestal, the archaeologist described the firing process: a glossy slip had to be painted over the figures' silhouettes, which would turn black in the kiln, while the unvarnished background turned a burnt red.

For each line in the figures' bodies—blank eyes, hilts of swords, gaping wounds and mouths—incisions had to be scraped into the slip, allowing the red of the ground to show through. The writer admired this symmetry: wherever the soldiers slashed at their victims with swords, the artist had to slash at their silhouettes with a stylus. It even put him in mind of the *giallo*, whose killer was also often visible in silhouette, a stabbing shadow on the wall. Whenever the blade cut into a victim, the film would cut as well, returning, after the edit, to their injured flesh, where a lurid line of red paint now gleamed. The writer was moved to imagine that this was the same red line as on these jugs, a two-thousand-year-long vein connecting seventh century Etruscan figures to 1970s Italian figures. The ceramicist and the cinematographer had been practicing the same art, he thought, scraping away at the same images, the one on jugs and the other on celluloid, both revealing the deep redness beneath things. For thousands of years, it seemed, the people of this region had been driving horrific images into each other's minds. Each generation of artists had continued to perfect the pictorial depiction of death, inheriting strategies of verisimilitude and passing them down in turn, across millennia and across media, from the mythological tableaux on these pots to the paintings of Christian martyrs, from the rows of cephalophore statues in the park—holding out their severed heads to passing joggers like poor beggars, panhandling with their brainpans—to the serial killer in the film, a never-ending nightmare of incisions, exoculations, and beheadings that had been haunting the Italian head and the Italian eyeball for all time. *Giallo* and this jug were just two guises of a single genius loci, the writer realized, as he watched the archaeologist circle the pedestal to take photos, notes. He found himself wondering what she would think of the film, if she watched it that night. Its hero was, like her, a kind of archaeologist: while investigating an abandoned house he thinks to chisel off the sheetrock, uncovering a bloodred fresco in one room (a child's stick-figure mural of the murderer), and exhuming a walled-up skeleton in another. On the walk back to the Academy the writer reminded everyone about his screening. But later that evening, as he waited in his studio, it grew clear that none of the scholars were going to come. The only fellows to show up were other artists—a composer, a photographer, a painter—and after delaying a while for the archaeologist, the writer pressed Play. The next day, at lunch, he sat at the archaeologist's table, alongside the same group of scholars from her tour. She asked how the screening had gone, and he told her, frankly, that she had missed a masterpiece. She was apologetic: I just can't stand horror movies, she said. All that violence— what's the point? The others murmured in agreement, and he shrugged understandingly. But inside he wanted to know: What was the point of the violence on her jug? In the weeks that followed, as he attended the other scholars' lectures, the question continued to trouble him. Whenever he looked to the archaeologist in the audience, her face always glowed with pleasure, hungrily absorbing whatever horror painting or horror sculpture was on display: the grisliness of Gentileschi's Judith, hacking away at Holofernes; the monstrous statues at Bomarzo; barbarians being slaughtered on a sarcophagus's relief. What was going on inside her mind, he wondered. Why this violence, and not that violence? What did she see here that she could not see in the *giallo*, or what did she see in the *giallo* that he could not see? Finally the night of her own lecture arrived, and as she calmly clicked through her slideshow, sharing graphic close-ups of her horror jug, the writer felt he was beginning to understand. Scholars must prefer old violence to new violence, he thought. The older the violence was, the more it must look like knowledge, to them. Just as fossils turn to oil in the earth, violence must turn to knowledge in its oldness. In the *giallo*, whenever the hero uncovers a violent fresco or a skeleton, he can still recognize, with dread, that it is an image of his own death he is seeing; whereas this was precisely the knowledge that the archaeologist was able to ignore, there on the ancient surface of her jug. The *giallo* had been released two thousand years too early for her to maintain this same distance from it, and so, in the meantime, she would go on studying pottery. Not Italian violence, only Etruscan violence. Amphora gore, yes; movie gore, no. She *refused to watch* 1970s black-gloved murderers, while she *devoted her life* to seventh century black-figure murderers. Maybe centuries from now, the writer imagined, an archaeologist would come to the Academy to conduct research on *giallo*. They might exhume a copy of the same film from a Roman landfill and deliver a packed lecture to the other scholars, pausing each death scene to explain its practical effects: prop blade, red paint, latex. By then anyone who might be frightened by the film—everyone in this room, for instance—would be gone. They would have long since joined the jug underground in the becoming of knowledge. This thought, more than anything he had seen or heard in Rome, was what did come to frighten the writer. He turned from the illustrated cadavers in the slideshow to the imminent cadavers around him. They were jugs, he thought. One day we will all be jugs. That was the true horror of the *giallo* film, if not of every horror film. With each stroke of the meat cleaver the murderer was sending living beings into the world of jugs, banishing them to a future when their skulls would hold no power and no terror. If he could watch this with pleasure now, it must be because his vision had already been invaded by that future: he was seeing today's deaths with tomorrow's eyes. The archaeologist proceeded through her slideshow, and he studied the grotesque details there freshly, seeing the jug as if for the first time. Just as centuries of dirt had had to be brushed from its surface, he could see centuries of seeing being scraped away from each new slide. Allowing the red of the ground to show through. He saw the stabbed soldiers, paused in the postures of their dying. The swords fixed forever in their flesh. He saw their mute mouths, crying out with pain but without sound. And the sight of it all—all that violence—disquieted him. This was how the jug must have looked, he understood, in the dawn of its making. When the first Etruscan laid eyes upon it, still glistening from the kiln, this was the horror it must have driven into them. He could see it clearly. He could not look away. And after the lecture had ended, and he returned to his studio, he found he could not sleep. He took out the *giallo* again. Maybe this time, he thought, he would be able to see what the archaeologist saw. Alone in the dark, centuries before those others who would come, he might be able to see it new, now, for the first time. The writer pressed Play and the horror began.

PORTONACCIO SARCOPHAGUS

IN THE PALAZZO MASSIMO MUSEUM IN ROME, I VIS-
ited the small dark room where the Portonaccio Sarcophagus is
kept. It was my last day in the city, after a year at the Academy,
and tomorrow I would be returning home. I was the only visi
tor in the room. The sarcophagus was spotlit from above, with
a row of cushioned stools before the tomb. Taking a seat in
the middle, I studied the minute details in the relief, an elaborate battle scene in which dozens of Roman soldiers trampled
barbarians from horseback, impaling them with spears. The
crowded composition filled the façade completely, from the
base of the sarcophagus to its lid, layered in horizontal bands of
bloodless bloodshed. The result was a dense thicket of bodies:

halfway up the frieze a horse's hooves might be draped over the shoulder of the soldier one row below, as he raised his arm to deliver a blow to a barbarian standing on a corpse one row below him, limbs tangled like this from corner to corner. I sat before the sarcophagus for many minutes, letting my eye rove slowly across the different strata of slaughter there. I wasn't sure how to read the frieze: whether the scene was meant to be taken in simultaneously, as a single moment, when the crush of opposing armies had formed a mounting heap of corpses; or else whether the viewer was meant to scan the scene sequentially, with each horizontal band representing a different phase of the battle as it unfolded across time, beginning at the top (where the barbarians were still upright) and ending at the bottom (where the Romans stood victorious on a carpet of vanquished combatants). Along the lid of the sarcophagus, above the battle, there was a separate frieze, portraying different moments from the life of the tenant entombed inside it. These vignettes had been arranged in a more straightforwardly linear way, in isolated groupings from left to right: in the lefthand vignette the dead man's wife educates their children; in the central vignette the dead man and his wife hold hands; in the righthand vignette the dead man makes a gesture of clemency over his conquered enemies. Despite their mundanity, something about these domestic scenes transfixed me, continually drawing my attention from the battle below. It was only after scanning them several times, my eyes passing repeatedly over the figures there, that I noticed the stray detail that must have been troubling me: both the dead man and his wife were faceless. Their heads were left blank, not just in one vignette but in all of them, and so—despite the fine detailing of their bodies, with fastidious folds carved into their garments—they lacked likenesses.

Once I had registered this it was the only feature I could focus on, and I marveled at how long it had taken me to notice. What made their facelessness even more conspicuous, in retrospect, was the fact that they were flanked by faces: the frieze was bookended by the crescents of two oversized gargoyle heads, each staring in opposite directions, such that the entire scene appeared to take place between parentheses, interjacent within a Janus whose doubled skull seemed—like a serpent's jaws—to have dislocated to contain it all. I turned around in my seat to read the wall text. The tomb's intended tenant, I read, had been identified in the scholarship as Pompilius: an official of Marcus Aurelius in command of two squadrons during the war against the Marcomanni (172–175 AD). Though he had had his name restored to him in death, his portrait had been left unfinished: The faces of the principal characters remained incomplete, the wall text read, awaiting the features of the dead people. Where their eyes and noses and mouths should have been, there were just smooth ovals of white marble, like eggs from which their deaths would hatch. Left uncarved, these featureless heads looked erased or eroded, and when I returned my attention to the battle scene, I saw that there was an effaced figure there as well. At the very center of the fray, raising his sword, a faceless if not headless horseman reared prominently (even his horse had a face, if a beast's snout and eyes can be described as a face. I cannot say, Levinas had said somewhere, I suddenly remembered, whether a snake has a face). Beneath the general's helmet there was only a melted-seeming mass of missingness: Pompilius. Elsewhere in the museum that day, I had observed a similar effect in damaged statues and weathered frescoes, where over centuries the figures' faces had flaked away syphilitically, or been chipped off by thieves, or else been condemned to oblivion in the defacement ritual known as *damnatio memoriae* (when universally loathed politicians were finally deposed, I had read, their public images were destroyed, every existing image of them—paintings, statues, even engravings of their names—symbolically abolished: in a bas-relief of a dozen men in togas, I had been moved to pity by the sight of a single memory-damned man in the middle, his pitted head surrounded by the smiling or frowning expressions of his companions; his features alone had been cursed, lost forever to the forgetfulness of the chisel, the prosopagnosia of the pickax). At first glance, Pompilius and his wife seemed to have suffered similar processes of decomposition, which rendered the frieze's celebration of their life—with two faceless shapes holding hands and rearing children—paradoxically ghostly, as though even in life they had already been dead. With their masks of flat stone, the figures seemed even deader—more purely dead— than the slain barbarians beneath them, for at least those crushed and grided bodies had been granted faces, however twisted in agony and hatred; and Pompilius and his wife seemed deader, too, than any skull would be, for a skull still has eye sockets and jaws and a nasal cavity, whereas these pebble-headed creatures on the sarcophagus's lid seemed to have been polished by death to a smoothness anterior to life, eroded down to the pale neutral beneath all being. In fact, however, the faces had not eroded, and the sarcophagus had undergone the opposite of decomposition. What had been preserved along the lid—what had been protected from decomposition—was non-composition itself. For two millennia the heads had been left unmarked. They were empty ground, blank in the way that undeveloped photographs are blank, as they await the faces that will rise out of them in the darkroom. Scrutinizing them more closely, I tried to imagine why they might have been left unfinished in the first place. It seemed improbable that a patron like Pompilius would have run out of money. Perhaps he had been superstitious, reluctant to commit his features to eternity during his own lifetime, for fear of courting Death, or perhaps the responsibility for completing the sarcophagus had fallen to neglectful or uncaring heirs. Pompilius's survivors—those friends and children whom he had had immortalized on his frieze—might have turned out to be derelict caretakers of his memory, I thought, traitors of his face, it was the task of every child to construct their parents' monument, memorial, or shrine, maintaining a frame in which they might be saved. The more I looked at them there, the more I found myself wondering about them, his children. When they visited this sarcophagus in the family crypt, to mourn their father and their mother, these planed faces must have been the only commemorating image that they were met with. And as the years drew on, I wondered, and as it became harder for them to remember their parents' features, would they eventually have come to feel admonished by these anonymous bossages gazing back at them, like gorgoneions of all they had forgotten? The mind displays qualities in the face, Marcus Aurelius had written, and so Pompilius's mind, too, must have fallen victim to this same forgetfulness, consigned to his face's fate in the memory of his mourners. Then again, if the sculptor had left the frieze unfinished, it was possible that no one had ever been buried here at all. The wall text made no mention of remains having been discovered inside, when it was excavated near Via Tiburtina in 1931. Part of the magnetism of the sarcophagus was likely owing to this fact: if it was an empty or unconsummated grave, the tomb must still be awaiting its corpses as those heads awaited their faces, which gave it the aspect of a warning. In the ghost stories I now taught for a living, the living routinely ignore such warnings, just as I would no doubt ignore Pompilius's warning to me, I thought, whatever it turned out to be, it is in the nature of such warnings that they can be recognized only in retrospect. As I was considering this, a woman my mother's age entered the room with her husband, and they sat on the stools next to mine. From the corner of my eye I watched her point out the uncanny non-faces on the lid, wondering aloud whether the sarcophagus had been sculpted on spec, rather than commissioned. If the central figures were meant to be anonymous, she reasoned to her husband, the tomb could be sold to anyone, with the identifying details added after the fact, customized to match the inhabitants. Just as a headstone could be sculpted in advance of any particular owner and engraved with their name once the time came, these stony heads might have been sculpted in advance of their patrons, whose own faces would be carved into them. After taking a few photos of the sarcophagus with their phones, the woman and her husband left. I remained seated, regarding the sarcophagus differently in light of what she had said. If she was right—if the sculptor had designed the tomb not for Pompilius in particular but for any paying customer— then the facelessness of the frieze's figures might mark the place of fungibility in death. Since everybody must die, any human face could occupy these bodies. Not just Pompilius and his wife, but any man and any wife. Even this man and his wife, I thought. My father and my mother. Any pair of strangers could be projected into the scenes represented on the lid. Whoever wanted to could educate the children, hold hands, bestow mercy on the barbarians. The faceless figures would function like those boardwalk cutouts that people pose inside for photographs: the shirtless muscleman beside the bikini-clad woman, both their heads hole-punched through with empty ovals. If you were to film a boardwalk cutout for an afternoon in time-lapse, I had often imagined, and watch the footage of passing tourists, you would see hundreds of faces streaking through the muscleman's head, one after another in an indistinct blur. The cutout alone would remain distinct, forming the stable framework through which these faces flashed. Meanwhile, in the interval between each mask, time-lapse would reveal the muscleman's true face: facelessness. An ovoid void, abyssal with blue sky, or foggy with passing cloud. It was no different, I thought, with the figures in this frieze. If Pompilius and his wife had been buried in the sarcophagus, their features would have been added to the blank heads on the bodies. But anyone else could fill that slot just as easily, displacing Pompilius from his portrait. Old features could be sanded off, new ones carved in their place. I pictured my own face there, my sisters', my mother's, that woman and her husband, until all our features canceled each other out in the confusion of smooth stone. Anyone could substitute Pompilius in his tomb, for the tomb is, after all, the ultimate site of substitution, that place where all faces are the same and all identities can be exchanged, where all mortal differences between individuals decompose. Death is just the stable framework, the cutout structure, within whose void a million mortal faces blur. It was even possible to view the faceless figures as a portrait, not of Pompilius, but of this blur itself: as if every person who had ever died—Pompilius and his wife, the slain barbarians below them and the forgiven barbarians beside them, even their children and the sculptor too—had been overlaid on the blank heads, as if all these faces were contained inside Pompilius's facelessness. Condensed in it. This condensation in death is the state that Nietzsche had been able to reach in life, I recalled, when, during the mental breakdown that he suffered in Turin near the age of fifty, he declared in a letter: I am Prado, I am also Prado's father, I venture to say that I am also Lesseps... I am also Chambige... every name in history is I. Looked at this way, each unnamed blank head on the façade simply was this every name in history. Just as the battle scene below had collapsed an entire military campaign into a single simultaneous catastrophe—with horses layered over barbarians layered over soldiers, all of them piling up in a temporal labyrinth of limbs—so too had the featureless heads above them, I thought, collapsed the past into a single moment. For if the myriad faces of the collective dead were to be superimposed one on top of the other, compressed into the palimpsest of a common death mask, this was what they would look like: a whorl of unscored marble. Staring at them now, I remembered a photo that my mother had taken when she visited Rome. She had traveled to Europe only once in her life, on a two-week trip with a friend, to celebrate her fiftieth birthday. They had also visited Berlin, Dublin, London, spending a few days in each city. This was near the turn of the millennium, and she had brought a disposable camera for the trip. When she returned home she dropped off the camera at the one-hour photo at the CVS, and after the roll had been developed—the pictures, I remember, were printed on glossy postcard stock and stacked together in a fat blue envelope—my older sisters and I had spent a night looking through them with her, fanning them across the coffee table in the living room. The only image that has stayed with me, in the two decades since that night, was the snapshot of our mother and her friend in an Italian cemetery.

They are posing beside an illegible headstone: the name cannot be made out in the engraving, and to this day I do not know who is buried there. The site had been her friend's suggestion, and by the time she returned home our mother could not recall where the cemetery was, or why they had stopped to take the photo there in the first place, or who had taken it for them, of course she would not be able to remember now. But once the picture had been developed, the grave was no longer its true subject. What drew everyone's attention instead, that night, was the faceless figure that had materialized beside the headstone. Standing just over our mother's shoulder—and unmistakably staring down at her—is the iconic figure of the Grim Reaper, an anthropomorphic shade in a black hooded cloak. His wide cowl obscures his head, and all that is visible within the shadow there—no grinning skull; no pale white corpse's face—is a numinous fog. There floats a wisp of blurred purple, like incense smoke or dry ice. My mother's camera would have been the cheapest available disposable Kodak—one of those yellow cardboard boxes with a crude automatic flashbulb, and a crummy thumbwheel of crenulated plastic that had to be wound after every snapshot to slide the filmstrip into place—and we speculated that it must have malfunctioned. Maybe the thumbwheel had been improperly wound, resulting in a double exposure, or maybe the film had been damaged in the developing tray at the one-hour photo lab, resulting in a chemical stain. Whatever the explanation, we dismissed this black blotch as an artifact of the photographic process, a maculation that we could misrecognize as Death only because of its morbid context. The fact that it was standing beside a headstone primed us to see it as a specter, whereas if this same blotch had materialized on any other photo from the trip, appearing beside Big Ben or the Berlin Wall (or even if it had been positioned anywhere else in this same photo, floating sideways in the sky for example), we might not have given it a second thought. That night, though, as we passed the photo around, my sisters and I teased our mother mercilessly about her phantom. It's Death, we told her, he's coming for you.

Or else, we said, it's the ghost of whoever was buried there: he sabotaged the picture to punish you, for disrespecting his resting place and trespassing over his grave. Ooh, our mother said, spooky, and next we accused her of staging the photograph as a prank. For the black blotch really did look embodied, three-dimensional. It had none of the flatness of an artifact, it looked like a man in a shroud physically standing there. We asked whether she had been on a haunted tour of Rome. Was this their tour guide in a Grim Reaper costume, posing for souvenir photographs with the group? No, she said, there was no one else there, they had stood alone beside the headstone that day. And in truth it was obvious that this presence could not be a human in any costume. There was something too unearthly about the purple blur beneath the cowl, it was too unlike light or life. With

a magnifying glass my sisters and I were able to make out the faintest pareidolic details of a devil's expression in the distortion: we could see eyelike depressions that seemed narrowed in a glower; the lines of a possible cheekbone, nose, brow; two upcurving curls of purple protruding from the forehead like horns. We were deceiving ourselves, we knew, the fog was featureless, but we strained to find a face within it. We never did determine the technical source of the effect: lens flare, overexposure, chemical reaction. What it reminded me of more than anything were the digitally blurred faces from the horror film *The Ring*, which had been released the previous year and which had left a deep impression on me, long after I had left the theater. When characters in this film watch a haunted video tape, they are doomed to die within seven days, and one symptom of this curse is that their faces can no longer be photographed. In every picture taken of them their faces alone—not their bodies or their clothes—appear distorted and whorled. This glitch seems to foreshadow the eventual fate of their physical faces in the film, for when a victim's seven days have expired a ghost comes to claim them, literally frightening them to death, and their corpses are discovered with grotesquely fear-twisted expressions. In the days beforehand, this same distortion can be glimpsed in pictures of them. As soon as the curse attaches to them, the camera receives static interference from their futures: it captures them not as they are in the moment, but as they will be in seven days, when their faces have been estranged by death, fright, decomposition. The whorl in the photograph is like a portal or a peephole through time, allowing you to peer through their present face into their future face, through their mortal face into their posthumous face, I cannot say whether a ghost has a face. What transfixed me about this blurring effect when I first saw the film, staring up at it alone in the dark room of the theater, was the way that the curse managed to invert the paradox of photographic time. For what was typically uncanny about old photographs was the way that they could show you the living faces of people who had long been dead: even if the subject had died a century ago, they continued to regard you from a moment before their death, when their death still lies (and will always lie) years or decades in their future, which was why when looking at an old photograph it was possible to think the paradox, He is dead, and he is going to die. *The Ring*'s cursed photographs reversed this formula, showing you the dead faces of people who were still alive. The prophetic or proleptic glitch in the camera served to implant their future seven days in their past, like a stain that had leaked backward through the week. This had the effect of shifting the tense of the paradox, from a simple future to the future anterior: looking at their image, you were able to think, He is going to die, and he *will have been* dead. Even as a teenager I recognized that this horror trope—the camera that photographs the future—was a stock device, a cliché (I had encountered it already as a child in the *Goosebumps* book *Say Cheese and Die!*, whose cartoon cover featured a premonitory Polaroid of a cheerful skeleton in a chef's hat and apron grilling at a backyard barbecue). But when I saw *The Ring*, those masks of erasure impressed me as an authentically unnerving image of negative portraiture. Whereas most portraits represented an attempt to defeat death and preserve the subject's likeness, extending their presence forward through time, these photographs preserved instead death's defeat of portraiture: what was extended backward through time was the subject's future absence in time, not their likeness but their lostness, their inevitable facelessness in death. *Damnatio memoriae.* This image of memorylessness had remained, strangely, the most memorable image from the film for me. Even now, whenever I descended into Street View in Google Maps, I was reminded of it: there any stray pedestrians, bystanders who happened to have been photographed by the surveyor van's panoramic roof-mounted cameras, have their heads pixelated for privacy, and the flesh-toned fog that the facial-recognition algorithm employs—a cloudy smudge of digital condensation, like breath on a mirror—never failed to recall the whorl effect from the film. The resemblance was so strong that no matter where I found myself in Street View, whether I was exploring Rome or my childhood neighborhood back home, I always felt as if I were really inside *The Ring*, navigating a world where every passing pedestrian has been cursed (the way that these blurred figures are all frozen mid-stride, statuefied, gives one the creeping sensation of wandering through a ruin: the landscapes evoke a prosopagnosic or Portonaccian apocalypse, in which everything has been preserved through petrifaction *except* faces, like some Pompeii of Pompiliuses). It was the same with our mother's photograph. As I looked at it that night, studying the violet distortion beneath the reaper's cowl, confronted there with the literal facelessness of Death, I had the impression that we had somehow entered *The Ring*. She is doomed to die, I could not help thinking. I didn't believe that the photograph had the power to haunt her, or to bring about her death. But I did believe that her death would have the power to haunt the photograph. As long as she was alive, my sisters and I would be able to joke about the specter, but if in the following week or weeks our mother were to be struck down by a car, the meaning of the photograph would shift. It wasn't just that we would look at it differently, no longer able to fully dismiss the hooded figure. We would likewise *remember* it differently: those weeks in which we had laughed it off would now seem—in retrospect—charged with anticipation. The picture had always been a premonition, we would realize, it had always presaged her fate. Her death would have contaminated the photo from the future, inflecting it with a future anterior, such that we would never be able to see it (or remember having seen it) in the same way. Whereas before it had been a joke, from there on out it *will have been* an omen. My mother did not die in the following week or weeks. Neither did her friend. Decades had passed since the picture was taken, and our mother was still alive. The photograph remained forgotten in her home, framed on a high shelf in the dining room's built-in bookcase, between her wedding photos and our graduation portraits, where I only ever glanced at it on holiday visits. Otherwise I could go months without its crossing my mind. In my time in Rome, city of memento mori, I had not thought of the photograph all year. I did not think of it in the catacombs, or at Keats's unmarked grave (Here lies one whose name was) under the shadow of the white pyramid of Cestius. I did not think of it in the Capuchin Crypt, where the skulls of hundreds of monks encrusted the walls like coral reef, and where a placard warned the living visitors: What you are now we used to be; what we are now you will be. It was only in the Palazzo Massimo, studying the ovals where Pompilius's face should be, that I was at last reminded of this image. I took out my phone and snapped a few photos of the tomb. Pinching the screen, I zoomed in on each faceless head until, magnified, they began to remind me even more strongly of our mother's specter. They really did bear a family resemblance, and it occurred to me that the hooded figure's facelessness might even fulfill the same function: like these ovals of unmarked marble, like the hole in a boardwalk cutout, the cowl might mark the place of fungibility in death. The empty slot that every face must blur through. In the past, whenever I had fantasized the photo metamorphosing as in *The Ring*, that was how I had pictured the curse's consummation: if this were a horror movie, I had imagined, our mother's face would eventually fade from her own head in the photo, leaving behind a blank space, and her features would materialize within the cowl's purple cloud, blurred there and barely visible. By that we would know the curse was complete: the photo had undergone its final change, her face had been developed in the darkroom that death will be (will have been). By now our mother had outlived the omen for so long that I no longer bothered with these fantasies. Even if she died tomorrow, I thought, before I flew home, her death would not make me view the photograph any differently. She would not die tomorrow. She was still physically healthy (she still took her long walks every morning), it was only her mind that was in decline. And it was at the thought of this decline—as I sat before the empty sarcophagus, awaiting the features of the dead people— that I did begin to view the photograph differently. It had been taken two decades ago, in a past she had no access to. If we were to show her the image now, I reflected, she would not be able to remember that afternoon in the cemetery, or the trip itself, she might not even recognize the friend beside her. Who is that, she would ask us, her companion as much a stranger to her as the specter. The photograph would remind her of nothing, or remind her at most that she could no longer be reminded. Whereas for me the image would remain layered with memories—of her, her friend, her face, of my sisters and of that night, and of this afternoon, too, I could tell: this room in the Palazzo Massimo would be contained inside the photograph as well, from now on—for her it could only be an image of her own memorylessness. In the time that I had been abroad, my sisters had informed me, her condition had been deteriorating. Afternoons, over FaceTime, they updated me on her progress. How she had begun to call my youngest sister by my oldest sister's name. How, midway through lunch with her own sister, she had forgotten who it was she was eating with: when our aunt tried to remind her, she grew alarmed and cried out—loud enough to attract the ministrations of the restaurant's manager—You're not my sister, who are you, you're not my sister. How a neighbor had found her at the CVS, withdrawing money from an ATM for a stranger, who had claimed—when the neighbor questioned him—that our mother was paying him the hundred she owed him. How last week she invited another stranger into the house—he convinced her he was my childhood friend—and let him sleep in my bed for the night. She had been living alone since our father had died, and my sisters had been doing what they could as her caretakers. They had installed a security camera above her doorbell to monitor her, a motion-activated surveillance device called the Ring, whose inconspicuous pinhole lens began recording the moment that anyone approached. It streamed the footage live, uploading brief clips to a cloud account that my oldest sister managed. Most of the footage was incidental: the mailman, a canvasser, our mother leaving for her morning walk or returning home. When unlocking the door, she often scowled at the lens suspiciously, having forgotten what it was or who had put it there, and sometimes she even brought her eye to it, as though it were a peephole into the house (watching these clips in Rome, streaming her face from the cloud days or weeks after it had been uploaded there, I had the impossible sensation that she was the one watching me: it felt as though she were peering through the lens and the laptop screen into my room, into my future). It was only because of the Ring that we had learned about the latest incident—with the overnight guest—at all. By the time we saw the footage, the following day, he had already left, and our mother had no memory of his having stayed there. In the clip itself she never appears in the frame, can only be heard as a disembodied voice off-screen. Do I know you? Do you know my son? Yeah I know your son. We went to school together. Of course, that's right. You must have gotten a haircut, I almost didn't *recognize* you. Come in. According to my sisters, these episodes of misrecognition had only been multiplying while I had been in Rome. They worried it was no longer safe for her to live alone. It may be time, they kept saying, to think about a home. I didn't disagree with them, though misrecognition now struck me, for the first time, as the wrong word for what she must be experiencing: what it must be like, inside her mind, during those first moments of confusion. Regarding the blank heads before me, trying to imagine her opening the door to this stranger, I wondered whether this frieze's eerie featurelessness might be closer to what now haunted her. Maybe it wasn't just that she failed to recognize people's faces, I thought: without memory, she must inhabit a world without faces. Figures must approach her with heads like blurs, indistinguishable until they have identified themselves. Every face must remain blank until it has laid claim to a name. Before that moment they were simply every name in history. I could almost imagine this, because it was the way that faces behave in dreams (dreams being, like death, that other space where identities undergo condensation: you might be speaking with your colleague until she announces that she is your dead father, and then it is your father you are speaking with). The face shifting to accommodate its new name. No, Mom, I'm your other daughter. Your sister. I am Prado, I am also Prado's father, I venture to say that I am also Pompilius, your son's friend. Where's that hundred you owe me? Features emerging as if from smooth stone. Yes, that's right, I remember now. How silly of me. Did you get a haircut? Perhaps that was the true meaning of the photo's omen, I thought. Maybe what the graveside specter had been presaging was not her future death but her future disorientation, her banishment to this maze of facelessness. I had always pictured her own features being displaced onto the purple blur, but this, I was coming to understand, had been the wrong cliché. Instead it was as if the purple blur had itself been displaced, overflowing from beneath the cowl to surround her in life, superimposed over the heads of everyone she encountered. Now people approached her as the dead do, or figures in dreams, all faceless and changeable. No sooner had I imagined this than I realized that the underworld I was picturing, this so-called maze of facelessness, was merely a version of Street View. A vision came to me of our mother embarking on her long walks each morning, staring at foggy neighbors as they waved at her, each of them as unplaceable as the apparitions in the map. In the past week, since the last time I'd spoken with my sisters, I had taken to entering her address into Google Maps and descending into Street View. To do this I had to select Pegman, the faceless orange ragdoll in the bottom corner of the screen, and drop him in front of her house. This shifted the camera from the aerial two-dimensionality of the map to a first-person three-dimensional perspective, allowing me to control Pegman with the arrow keys. Setting out from her house, I would head to the lakes and back, recreating the route of her walks. I didn't know what I hoped to accomplish. I had the nagging thought that I might find her there: that she might have been one of the pedestrians captured by the camera van, when it had last surveyed the neighborhood (according to the timestamps, two years earlier). A form of superstition,

I supposed, magical thinking, at some level I must have hoped that, if she could not live on her street anymore, at least she might live on in Street View, that the map might be her monument. Searching for her, I was struck anew by the apocalyptic stillness of Street View. Leaves do not quiver on their branches. Shadows are frescoed to the concrete. Cars sit in the middle of the road, as if abandoned. The unremarkable motionlessness of every photograph is rendered strange, there, by my own motion through it, my ability to navigate the stasis. Pegman alone is unpaused, free to wander where others are fixed, an interloper in this frozen world (perhaps this was why Google had designed his body as a puffy orange parka, I thought, in everything he was proportioned like an astronaut suit: the helmet-shaped head, the insulated limbs, the barrel torso. The design implied maximum protection against inhospitable environments: in order to explore the durational depths of the photograph—a moment dilated to eternity—Pegman first had to be pressurized with time, helmeted with it. Again I was reminded of the hooded visitor in the cemetery, as though this specter had itself been a kind of Pegman, an irreption into the image from an alien temporality). I never did find her. Though I recognized many of her neighbors, blurry figures out jogging or walking their dogs— like Pompilius's horse, their pets retained their faces—our mother was nowhere to be seen. At the time I had experienced this as an obscure disappointment, a vanishment in advance of death: Street View was one more place that would forget her, I thought, one more crypt in which she would lack a commemorating image. But now I could see the consoling or compensatory side of things. For I had been searching Street View, I realized, not merely for her but as her. The view of the street

90

that I had been afforded was, in a way, her own: whenever I wanted to I could retrace her steps there, encountering this land of ghosts—blurry, half-familiar—as she might have found it. Over a hidden loudspeaker there came a disembodied voice, announcing first in Italian and then in English that the museum would be closing soon. I rose from the stool, taking a few final photos: of the wall text, the sarcophagus, Pompilius. Leaving the tomb and the room behind me, walking back to the Academy for the last time, I thought about my long flight home. For the week that I would be there my sisters had scheduled visits to several facilities, and they had suggested that now would be the time for me to take stock of her house, boxing up any belongings or photographs that I wanted to save. They would be picking me up from the airport tomorrow, and our mother would be with them. It had been over a year since she had seen me in person. I expected her still to recognize me. And if she didn't? If she failed at first to place me? At least I will have known, by the confusion in her eyes, something of what she was seeing, as she watched her daughters embrace this stranger. As he turned to introduce himself, and did his best to compose my face.

AFTERLIVES

THEY VISITED SICILY THAT WEEKEND. BOEING crashes were in the news, so throughout the flight over the Mediterranean their talk was of turbulence, burial at sea. Driving into Palermo, he paused at a memorial beside the highway, an obelisk monument to the 1992 Capaci bombing, when the Mafia had packed thirteen drums of Semtex and TNT beneath the road and remotely detonated them under a judge's motorcade. Local seismographs, she read aloud from her phone, had registered the explosion as an earthquake. Later, at lunch, talk turned to respect for the dead: soldiers recovering fallen bodies from battlefields; mountaineers carting down frozen climbers' corpses. He cited Antigone's fidelity to Polyneices, sprinkling earth over his cadaver to short-circuit its state-mandated fate as carrion, food for dogs and vultures. Would you do that for *me*? she asked. He thought about it. He had never been sentimental about funerary rituals. It made no difference to the dead, was his feeling. After he died, the career of his corpse—whether it was buried, burned, exposed to scavengers; whether left at sea, or on a mountainside, or on the side of a Sicilian highway—would be a matter of no consequence to him. He certainly wouldn't want her to get herself killed recovering it. But when he considered what he would realistically do in the same situation—for instance if they were stranded in an apocalyptic wasteland, he imagined, and one afternoon she was late coming home, and at sunset he noticed a weird scrum of wild dogs in the distance, and raising his binoculars he saw that what they were all fighting over was her corpse—his eyes surprised him by watering, not in the daydream but in reality, there at the restaurant. He described the dog scenario to her. Yes, he said, if I found a pack of wild dogs devouring your dead body, I think it would enrage me. I would kick them off you and try to bury you. That's the sweetest thing you've ever said to me, she said. But what if—he knew what she was going to ask before she asked it—what if it weren't wild dogs? What if it were a pack of shar-pei puppies? Shar-peis were his family pet, his favorite breed. He loved to kiss their chubby, wrinkled cheeks. Often, to cheer him up while they were at work, she texted him GIFs of shar-peis. The last had been a looping clip of a shar-pei attempting to eat a strawberry off a hardwood floor: its cheeks were so heavy that they draped like theater curtains over the narrow aperture of its mouth, and each time it reared forward to snap at the strawberry its jowls made contact long before its jaws did, knocking the fruit across the floor like a hockey puck. He pictured a pack of puppies trying to nibble at her like this, as stymied by her remains as by the strawberry. If it were shar-peis, he admitted, I might just say, She's in a better place now. A better *place*?! Yes, he said, and why not a better place? Wouldn't you rather be buried in a puppy than a pyramid? But as soon as he said this he was struck by an eerily vivid mental image of a shar-pei: the dog was staring off in profile, solemn, the image in black and white. The camera of his mind's eye zoomed in on the dog's face, until gradually its gray cheek had filled the frame, then kept zooming in farther, magnifying its wrinkles to abstraction; seen up close, the wrinkles became a network of deep crevasses, with the multicursal lininess of a maze, and as the zooming camera approached this maze he could make out a human figure far below in it, a pale shape stumbling through one of the corridors with arms outstretched, and when finally the camera descended into this trench, bringing the trapped figure into focus, he saw that it was her, lost, distraught, doomed to wander like a flea through the cheek-flab labyrinth of the Leviathan who had swallowed her. He described what he had seen to her. It's a premonition, she said. Now you know what will happen if you feed me to shar-peis. I'll haunt you so bad. They left the restaurant and spent the weekend in archaeological parks, scrambling over the ruins of ancient temples and theaters, climbing collapsed column drums like boulders. On their last afternoon, driving back to the airport, they paused to admire a work of land art along the highway. A quilt of immense concrete blocks had been cast down a hillside, two acres of white rectangles with a network of narrow pedestrian paths running through them. Known as *The Great Crack*, she read aloud from her phone, the piece had been constructed as a memorial to the 1968 earthquake, which had leveled the town of Gibellina, killing hundreds. The concrete blocks had been cast according to the layout of the city: the gridded paths mapped onto its roads and alleys, while the blocks—which had been infilled with rubble and furniture from the ruins—stood in place of its buildings. Gibellina's real ruins, collapsed houses and churches, were still visible around them, on the outskirts of the sculpture. And just down the highway was Gibellina's real cemetery, with its rows of mausolea, neighborhoods of squat concrete houses for the dead. They were the only people there. They approached the monument together, entering one of its pathways at random. The blocks rose as high as their heads on either side, and the alley stretched before them in an endless white corridor. Following her, running his fingers along the concrete, he felt like an ant crawling across a tombstone: if an ant descended into the inscription, he imagined—if it entered the canyon of a letter, suddenly funneled forward by the high granite walls of the alphabet rising around it—it would never realize that the path it was tracing was a dead name. She announced that she wanted to see the monument from above, so they climbed toward the top of the hill, where there was a lookout platform. But the grade was steep, and as they trudged upward he had to keep stopping for her. Eventually she called to him to go ahead. He hiked to the platform alone, arriving cold with sweat and out of breath. Turning back, he saw the alleys he had just passed through as a labyrinth of craquelure, black lines fissuring a white surface. He scanned the expanse and found her: a small dark figure, wending through a white trench. A chill of recognition passed through him. When she reached the platform, he did not wait for her to catch her breath. Do you remember my premonition? he asked. He described the vision he had had of her ghost, lost in a shar-pei's wrinkles. She nodded cautiously: Yes? He waved one hand over the maze beneath them. Oh my God, she said. We're dead, he said. I'm really here, she said. It really ate me. We're dead, he repeated, and we don't even know it. We'll never leave this place. Together they stepped off the platform and descended into the monument.

MINDS OF WINTER

1.

BLIZZARD THIS MORNING. I SIPPED COFFEE ALONE at the window, watching the snow fall. It was ten degrees, overcast, and the glass was ferny with frost. Fat frantic flakes were being buffeted about in broken circles. A game I liked to play when it snowed this hard was to isolate a drifting flake within the window frame, somewhere near the top of the pane, and try to keep track of it as it fell. While it veered left and right I would follow it in its descent, careful not to lose sight of it amid the visual noise of the pointillist flurry, until finally it had disappeared beneath the sill. Concentrating now on the upper frame, I let several rows of snow pass, then picked a flake more or less at random. It was crumblike and evidently weightless, staying aloft a little longer than the rest. Whenever I focused on a flake like this, I found that it ended up seeming more animate than the others. Whereas most of the snow drifted down lifelessly, in mindless free-fall—no more volitional than the motes that fizzed through the window's shafts of champagne sunlight—whatever flake I happened to be focusing on seemed to be flying of its own accord, charting a safe route through the blizzard. It was no different with this flake. I watched as it hovered, swerved, chandelled, and dove, with what seemed like the motivated agency of a moth, as if evading birds or bats, or else like a spaceship in a dogfight, I imagined, a miniature Millennium Falcon navigating this asteroid field of white crises. And the longer I followed it in its zigzag erratic path, the more sentient it seemed. When a fatter flake drifted toward it, threatening to collide head-on and subsume it through their mutual fusion, the smaller flake juked left and flew free at the last moment, to all appearances 'eluding' the larger one. It really was as if there were some preservation instinct inside the snow, guiding it away from the dangers of melting or merging: some will to survive or individual identity that this single flake—the white shell of a slight self—was careful not to forfeit to absorption. What was odd about this illusion of consciousness, to me, was that it could be maintained only if I concentrated on the snow. If I were to merely glance out the window, I knew, the seething, staticky activity of the blizzard would seem uniformly inanimate and randomized again. That discrepancy interested me. It was strange that paying attention to a flake should imbue it with any more personality—any more inner life—than a passing glance would. What it reminded me of were the different levels of deadness in a doll, the way that play could bestow degrees of personhood on a piece of plastic. In childhood, when my Kenner Han Solo figurine lay discarded on the carpet, it was utterly devoid of life. Not just dead but inorganic: insensate matter that had never been alive. But as soon as I picked it back up, he became wholly Han Solo, intrepid in his Hoth parka and boots: I could march him across the tundra of the comforter, or mash him into a grappling match with Boba Fett, and for the duration of this play he would remain conscious and agentive, filled with plans, desires, conflicts. Even if he 'died' in battle with the bounty hunter—even if I went *Pew! Pew!* while strafing him with Boba Fett's jetpacked cataphractic action figure, and somersaulted Solo's cadaver through the air— even so, the 'dead' Han Solo would still be less dead in my hand than the toy had been back on the carpet. As long as he was in

104

play, he was a person: he *had been* alive and was therefore still a he, rather than an it. Only when I tossed the toy aside, turning my attention elsewhere, would Han Solo revert to cold object-hood, suspended once again in the cryonics (the carbonite) of nonconsciousness. By holding him in my hand, I animated him: I transmitted some vital spark from my own mind to his body through the jumper cable of my touch. Perhaps that was what was happening with the snow right now, I thought, watching my flake pendulate through the air—like a spider swinging down its thread—as it drifted toward the windowsill. Merely by looking at one flake in particular, I could summon it from out of the depths of its crystalline insentience, animating it not with my hand but with my eye. Through this act of concentration and play, my own consciousness was rubbing off on the flake. For as long as I focused on it, it came to seem creaturely and vibrant, because it was stirring inside of—being stirred to life by—the ray of my paid attention. The same way that a doll will seem to walk when you manipulate it; or the way that a dead moth's wings will flutter when you blow on them, beating with borrowed vibrancy. That was what was happening when I watched the snow falling beyond my window. From out of the white totality a tiny whiteness had individuated itself: one flake in particular had emerged from the flurry as a fleck of awareness. It was like watching mind emerge from matter, the coming to consciousness of one monad within matter's white mindlessness. This was why you needed a theory of mind when watching snow, I thought. An epistemology of the blizzard. Just before the flake finally disappeared beneath the sill, it lingered a little on the air, as if to give me a parting glance, and when it had passed out of sight I imagined it landing somewhere on the ground below, its thinking extinguished in whatever cold heap absorbed it.

2.

In the blizzard's lull, the pine tree by the street was left crusted with snow. I studied it through the window. Thick powder had amassed on the flat upper surfaces of its branches, resulting in a precise two-tone color field: each bough was divided into a white band above, and below, greenish bark. The snow was so consistently applied across the bark that, in grasping for the exact contrast that it called to mind, I found myself visualizing cupcakes, doughnuts, cookies: that stark border where the pale glaze gives way to dark pastry. And for the first time I understood, after using the terms unthinkingly all my life, why sugared glazes were called icing, or frosting, in the first place. Staring at a dusted branch, I thought, 'The snow looks just like icing' or 'It's like frosting,' and it was only by routing my mind through the dumbness of that redundancy—the snow literally *was* ice, *was* frost—that I was able to travel backward through the metaphor, recovering its source. I had inadvertently applied the image to its origin, reproducing in reverse the exact same process of phrase-making that some baker must have gone through centuries before, when, meditating on a new confection one winter morning and searching for a term to coin for the technique, they glanced out their window and saw the white coating of snow spread evenly over earth or over the bark of a branch and thought to call the sugar paste 'icing.' I took out my phone and checked Wikipedia: this sense of 'icing' dated back to at least 1683, according to the OED; 1750 for 'frosting.' In this way, I thought, a three-hundred-year-old thought had just escaped from the snow. It was as if the patissier's perception— that moment of insight at the bakery window—had been frozen in the snow as much as in the figure of speech. And I had now glimpsed that same perception in the snow outside this window. Just as a thawing block of arctic ice will sometimes release some ancient illness—a Precambrian flu, preserved for millennia in its pockets of trapped gas—it was as if the snow, too, had released in its slow melting this metaphor from the mind of that patissier, the posthumous point of view of a patissier, off-gassing into the winter air the wordplay of a patissier who had been dead now for three centuries. This must be what people had in mind when they described language as a virus. Frosting, I thought, as I studied the pine tree, and it was this dead patissier's thought that I was thinking, passing through my eye and into my mind, infecting my gaze with an other's word from another winter.

3.

The window's muntins divided the glass into a grid of squares, which gave the view outside the appearance of a split-screen. This made the winter landscape seem discontinuous, fragmented, as if the window were broadcasting half a dozen video feeds of half a dozen different snowy streets simultaneously. In one, a sidewalk. In another, the pine tree. I had grown used to staring at split-screens lately, since I had been spending more and more of my days videoconferencing on Zoom, which gridded its users into a matrix of mini-squares. Now, at the window, I had the momentary sensation—a kind of afterimage of the application—that I was on a conference call with several snowfalls. And when the blizzard began to drive fresh flurries against the glass, whiting out each screen with static, it was as if every feed had gone dead at once. This whiteout reminded me— something I had found myself thinking often recently—that the split-screen would be the better editing technique for represent- ing a mind in mourning. In most films, I had noticed, the edit associated with mourning was usually montage. When a charac- ter is grieving, the viewer knows that this mental activity is tak- ing place by the montage that plays, a carousel of three-second memory clips excerpted from the bereaved consciousness. Each memory is typically suffused with honeyed light and scored with swelling cello: the lost one laughing on a swing set at sunset; the lost one walking toward a dappled river, looking back to smile into the camera; the lost one running fingers through golden wheat; et cetera. This rapid succession of imagery is meant to suggest the shuffle effect of mourning: the way that scenes of the lost one will flash into consciousness, in no particular order; the way that you are not in control of what gets recalled, but simply have to endure these stray images as they strobe over you. But what montage missed, I thought, was the simultaneity of these memories. In the most difficult moments of mourn- ing—when you were so overwhelmed with impressions of the lost one that you couldn't breathe—it didn't feel as if you were cycling through a string of linear memories, one after the other, distributed serially through time. Instead, it felt as if you were experiencing every memory at the *same* time. The memory of the lost one laughing on a swing set would flash into conscious- ness alongside the memory of the lost one walking toward the river, alongside every other memory of the lost one, these dis- crete instants from your life all flooding through the one-sec- ond-wide aperture of your time-bound consciousness. The

memories may be distinct, discontinuous, but they were pre-
sented to the mind simultaneously. And it was the impossibility
of processing all these memories at once that inspired panic
symptoms in the body—the inability to breathe, the ragged
heartbeat—since for a moment it felt as if you were going to
die, or go dead, as if more and more memories would keep filling your mind until, overloaded, it would white out. No montage, however rapid-fire and visually overstimulating, could quite
approximate this feeling of congested recollection. If any editing technique could, it might be the split-screen. Assuming that
a film really wanted to represent the felt experience of mourning, I thought, the screen could be divided into a grid like this
window, with each panel playing a different scene: the lost one
on the sidewalk side by side with the lost one below the pine
tree, just above the lost one on the snowy street. That way, the
film's viewer would be placed in the same perceptual position as
the film's mourner, since the mental effort required of the audience to make sense of this matrix of images (holding them all in
mind at once, synthesizing these dozens of different screens
and processing them as a kaleidoscopic whole) would mirror the
mental effort required of the mourner to make sense of grief's
matrix of memories (holding them all in mind at once, synthesizing dozens of different moments from a life and processing
them as a single kaleidoscopic loss). Confronted with this perceptual impossibility, the viewer—like the mourner—would feel
the imminent whiteout in their minds. Thinking about this again
before the window, I recalled that passage from *Postmodernism,
or, the Cultural Logic of Late Capitalism*, in which Fredric
Jameson describes a similar perceptual breakdown in the context of a video installation. In an art gallery, Jameson describes,

a film is being played on different television monitors throughout the room, some on the ceiling, some on the floors, forcing
the viewer to rotate in place in order to compass them all and
construct a mentally coherent model of the fragmented film. It
is a split-screen that has been distributed through space. Standing
in the gallery, Jameson writes, the viewer feels called upon to 'do
the impossible, namely, to see all the screens at once'; and since
perceiving in this way would require a completely different sen-
sorium (eyes in the back of the head, for instance), spaces like
these seem to challenge the viewer to mutate or evolve beyond
their present body, to—in Jameson's phrase—'grow new organs.'
What the gallery seems to grant the viewer, then, is a kind of
negative apprehension of these new organs: the fleeting sensation—through their felt lack or need—of what *it would be like*
to possess them. In the same way that a small child grasping at
a cabinet just out of reach is able to feel—in the gap of negative
space between their fingertips and the handle—what it will be
like when they are finally grown up and tall enough to reach it,
thereby anticipating the potentials of this future self, the viewer
in this gallery is able to feel—through their very failure to perceive the screens—the optical possibilities of a future body. The
video installation, as a design space, seems to be intentionally
oriented toward this future body: every awkwardly angled television screen is an affordance for the viewer's future organs, just
as the tall cabinet's handle is an affordance for the child's future
fingers. Perhaps it was the same, I found myself thinking, with
the experience of mourning. When that memory wall over-
whelms the mourning mind, resulting in a crash of amnesiac
static, perhaps what we are meant to apprehend is the possibility
of a future consciousness, a mind beyond our present mind,

which would actually be able to contain all these memories in their simultaneity, revolving the totality of the lost one's life inside itself—like a diamond held up to light—to consider its facets from every side. Isn't that what people meant when they described the deathbed experience of having your life flash before your eyes? When characters undergo this process in films, it is also usually represented as a montage. But now I wondered whether this too might look more like (assuming it 'looks' like anything) a split-screen. For what you were supposed to be able to see in this vision was the wholeness and oneness of your existence—the adjacency of every moment on a single plane: your death already present in your birth, your children already present in your childhood—such that your entire life could be compressed into a millisecond of multifaceted or matrical remembering. And since this moment would contain inside itself every memory you had ever formed, it occurred to me, it would also have to include all your prior memories of mourning. The lost one on the sidewalk, the lost one below the pine tree, the lost one on the snowy street: they would be there, too, inside your dying. Every memory you had recalled long ago, in your bereavement, would be returned to you now on your deathbed. Those stray images would once again strobe over you, except this time, I imagined, you would experience none of the mental strain or sense of panic you had in mourning, since by now your dying mind would have expanded to the point where it could perceive these memories—alongside every other instant you had lived—in serenity. You would now be capable of doing the impossible, of seeing all these screens at once. The earlier experience of your mind in mourning would have been just a foretaste of this deathbed experience: when the lost one's life first flashed before you, it would have been a preview of your own life flashing before you, since the lost one would be one more panel in the grid that would flash before you as you died (and perhaps that was why, in the most difficult moments of mourning, whenever your heartbeat intensified and you had difficulty breathing, it sometimes felt as if you were about to die. In a manner of speaking you *were* dying: you were being brought closer than you were ordinarily capable of approaching to the vortex of your deathbed mind, when the one-second-wide aperture of your time-bound consciousness would split open to admit the split-screen of every moment from your life). Just as Jameson's video installation served as the negative apprehension of a future body, perhaps mourning was a negative apprehension of this moribund body. Through your failure to process your memories of the lost one, you were able to intuit what it *would be like* to properly remember the lost one: in other words, what it will be like to die. Maybe all mourning is an affordance for your deathbed self, I thought, as the blizzard withdrew from the window and the street came back into view. Maybe the whiteout helps prepare you.

4.

As it raked the ground outside, the wind gathered up loose grains of snow, molding them into sinuous spindrifts that helped to disclose the paths of its laminar flows. This was the only way I could tell that a hard breeze was blowing. Otherwise the world beyond the window looked still. Late afternoon and the sky already darkening. Along the sidewalk I watched these white lines slithering over the concrete, writhing in place like the ghosts of snakes. Each creature was a collaboration of particle and wave, debris and current, holding together for seconds before the wind shifted again and they whipped out and disintegrated. Whenever a line vanished like this, an identical one would soon form to replace it, taking shape in seemingly the same spot. The same wind was blowing over the same bare place on the sidewalk, and it was possible to imagine that each spindrift was even composed of the same particles of snow: that the current was recirculating its flakes as quickly as the turbulence dispersed them, recycling them into new lines. It was difficult to describe. This dynamic disintegration and reincorporation of the spindrifts—the way that thousands of saltating grains could converge on an invisible vector, shed away like spray, then rejoin it—put me in mind of the Large Hadron Collider, or those CGI animations of water droplets circulating in cough or sneeze columns, where swirling flumes of red-and-blue spheroids (meant to symbolize aerosolized particles but somehow recalling playground ball-pit balls) are slowed down and rewound, until their ostensibly stochastic trajectories can be mathematized and made imaginable. Like these phenomena, the spindrifts seemed to follow a chaotic process: something that could not be described in words, only modeled. But no sooner had this idea occurred to me than I realized that the gathering action of the wind was also, at bottom, syntactical. The wind was arranging its grains the way a sentence arranges its words, or a mind its thoughts, and each spindrift was as frangible as thought, too, falling apart as easily as a sentence does. I watched the lines outside vanish and reform. It was as if there were something the wind wanted to say and kept erasing. It was trying to get it right. It was difficult to describe. In a sense what I was watching was this very difficulty of description—the problem of indescribability—in motion. And so maybe the most faithful description of the spindrift would simply be to say that it resembled description itself. In any process of revision, the same sentence will need to keep being rewritten. The moment one version is erased—one wrong phrase—a minor variation will form to take its place. The same words keep occurring. Returning. They get caught in the current or breath of the sentence, drawn back into it, such that the line is trapped traveling the path of all its past attempts. Writing in place like the ghosts of snakes. Watching one spindrift slither, I wanted to say that the line writhes in place. Place was not quite right. I wanted to say that out of nothing, writhing, the line takes shape. I wanted to say the line writhes out of shape. The spindrift was soon erased, and the new line writhing looked like my own wanting to say. On the sidewalk outside, a wanting to say was taking place. What I wanted to say about its want to say was the way it was wanting to say in place. Even as I was watching this, the wind must have died down, or moved on, because all the spindrifts disappeared together, and the sidewalk went instantly white and flat, the surface smoothed like water calming. Along the curb, where the city's plows had shoveled up crusty mounds, I could make out faint striations in the hillocked snow, little ridges that the wind had carved and the cold had hardened. For a moment these scale-model sastrugi looked like spindrifts that had been solidified, frozen in time. The streetlamps ticked on just then, and all the snow beyond the window went neon in the orange light. It was difficult to describe.

INTRODUCTION TO THE READING OF HEGEL

The fact that a man has decided to *read* the *Phenomenology*
proves that he loves Philosophy.
—Alexandre Kojève, *Introduction to the Reading of Hegel*

THAT NIGHT THE READER COULDN'T READ. HIS
application for the Fellowship was due tomorrow at midnight,
and he still hadn't written his proposal letter. He'd gone to the
library to work, choosing his usual carrel on the top-floor stacks
and opening his laptop to the blank document. Since arriving he
hadn't seen another soul, and it had been so long since even he
had stirred that the track lights above the bookshelves—all
motion-activated—had clicked off one by one. The aisles spread
out before him in paths of darkness. Through the window
beside him—a tall pane embrasured into the brick, narrow as an
arrow-slit—he commanded a view of the campus parking lot. It
was December, deadline season, the trees were bare and the air
was gray, and though no snow was falling tonight, yesterday's
lines of white were still visible across the lot, making faint minus
signs of the concrete parking chocks. The library was quiet and
the world was calm. Six stories below, miniature students in
bright parkas headed to their parked cars, evening seminars,
bars. Some were probably his own students, the freshmen forced
to take his section of Introduction to Philosophy: it was the
same adjunct class he had been teaching for years, granted to
graduate students for a meager living stipend, usually enough to

cover the reader's rent and, in alternating weeks, either books then food or food then books. He had taught his last class today, held his last office hours, and his students had all turned in their final essays, which were waiting in his backpack for him to grade. Now they were free. For the rest of the break he would have the building—the books—to himself. He sipped black coffee from his Thermos. Dear reader, the reader deleted. To the members of the Fellowship committee, the reader deleted. Everything depended on the first sentence, he knew. The Fellowship was selective, and his reader or readers would be looking for any reason to reject him. At his first mistake they would stop. It was their *job* to reject, they were basically being paid to hate every applicant except one. He closed his eyes and tried to imagine them. The way that criminal profilers must cast themselves into the thoughts of the serial killers they track, he attempted to project himself into his rejector. How would a mind that isn't mine read this, he always asked himself when writing. How would this read to someone who isn't me, who doesn't know me? This is a good sentence, he sometimes caught himself thinking, but then, when he reread it with this other reader in mind—with this other reader's mind—he would think, This is a terrible sentence, and delete it. The Fellowship committee usually included former Fellows, one from each field, so the reader's reader would probably be one of his philosophical predecessors. He just had no way of knowing which one. For the past month, instead of working on his dissertation, he had been researching the Fellowship, refreshing its website hourly and clicking the link labeled Meet This Year's Judges, where he was always met with the same message: This year's judges haven't been announced yet, please check again soon. By now it was clear that the judges wouldn't be revealed until after the deadline. Before midnight tomorrow their minds would remain a blind spot, which made it impossible to write with them in mind. Everything about the Fellowship was kept shrouded in mystery like this. Even the building itself—centuries old, walled-in atop the highest hill at the heart of the capital—was a blind spot: its inner workings were as unknowable, as concealed from view, as the metamorphic core of a cocoon, that silk-lined space where change takes place. All the reader knew about it was that people emerged from it altered. Every year a dozen so-called *emerging minds* were permitted to enter it—emerging artists, scientists, and philosophers, emerging archaeologists and cartographers—and by the time they left its chambers they were no longer emerging but had emerged, they had somehow been transformed into real artists, real scientists, real philosophers. This was the only thought that enabled him to ignore the odds against him. He wasn't naive. He knew where the average Fellow was emerging from, they weren't crawling out of philosophical burrows or philosophical ditches but, almost always, were being hatched from the most rarefied philosophical incubators and the most prestigious philosophical chrysalises (at least a quarter came from N—). Still, he had found a few encouraging exceptions, ordinary readers like him. They must have been selected by dint of their erudition, he imagined. They must have been smarter, better read, than the other applicants that year, the intelligence in their letters must have been undeniable and therefore unrejectable, and so the only thing the reader could safely assume about his own reader or readers was that they would be using this same erudition metric to evaluate him: *they* would be scrutinizing *his* letter to determine how smart and well read *he* was. Knowing this had not been much help. In the weeks that he had been coming to this carrel, facing this blank document, he hadn't made any progress. Or—if it wasn't true that he'd accomplished nothing—the only progress he'd made had been epistemological. He hadn't written the first sentence, but he'd imagined the kinds of minds that might read the first sentence. While his letter remained empty (of words), it had become full (of these other minds): night after night as he had stared at it he had stored inside it all the different reasons that a reader might reject him. Whenever he typed a sentence, he tried to read it with eyes of skepticism and contempt. He read it out loud. He read it backward. He read it backward out loud. In the end he always deleted it. In his first draft of his first sentence, for instance, he'd written the phrase *comprised of* (as in, *My project is comprised of…*): he had reread the sentence a dozen times without registering the error, before it finally occurred to him to look up *comprised of*, and with dread he read a usage entry discouraging the phrase. It was considered nonstandard, and he'd almost let it stand. If he hadn't thought to check, and if one of this year's judges had turned out to be a grammar pedant, they would have stopped reading then and there. He deleted the phrase, typed *composed of*, deleted that as well. It had been the same every night. One first sentence had used *kind of* twice, another had used *I* three times. Last night he thought he had been making progress until he noticed the adjective *seminal*. He had described a philosophical concept as *seminal*, but once he read the sentence backward out loud—once he had begun to chant *lanimes lanimes* under his breath at this carrel—he was at last able to hear how *seminal* might sound to another reader, could appreciate how for certain readers the sheer appearance of *seminal*—the fact that a male applicant seemed to be praising the semen of a philosophical concept, its sperm count or motility or whatever—would be a red flag, a shibboleth, reason enough to reject him. There might be as many as a thousand other applicants for the Fellowship. Only one would cross the threshold, while the other nine hundred ninety-nine would all perish on the way, for defects as minimal as *seminal*. The odds could even be described—if you didn't already know better—as seminal. The reader had deleted *seminal* and started over, ending the evening with the same blank document he was faced with now. Well, not precisely the same. He wouldn't repeat his past selves' mistakes. He'd modeled these other readers' minds inside his mind, and now they were here with him, within him, watching over him. The *comprised of* hater, the *seminal* hater: his consciousness was a commons of all possible contempts. His temples pounded, he sipped more coffee. The metabolic costs of simulating other minds was high, he knew. To revise, you had to be able to cognize being watched, to be able to think the thought, *So this is how I look to them.* Ethologists had determined, the reader had read somewhere, that only a few nonhuman species could pass the so-called mirror test. If researchers painted a bright dot on an animal's forehead, then placed the animal before a mirror, only a few nonhuman species would recognize their reflection, reaching up to their own head to try to touch the dot or titivate themselves. This was essentially, the reader realized, a revision process. To erase a mistake on the body, an animal had to see themselves as another animal's mind would see them. He studied his reflection in the laptop screen. He'd switched the document to dark mode, typing white on black, and in the shadowy glass he could see his face. The cursor—a flashing white line—

blinked steadily in his head, pulsing near his temple like a panicked vein. He raised his hand to it, as though to brush it away, and this gesture was what separated him from dogs (but not the Asian elephant) and most birds (but not magpies), it was what elevated him above the invertebrates (except for cleaner wrasses) and enabled him to write this letter, addressing his mind to a mind he had never met. *Comprised of. Kind of. Seminal.* Revision was just a mirror test. Before you could write a worthwhile sentence, you had to become the sentence's nemesis. You had to occupy the place of a predatory or an editorial consciousness, hating yourself before the other had a chance to, to spare them the hatred altogether. There was no more absolute an act of empathy, the reader had always thought. Whenever he read a writer's sentence that he hated, he knew that what he was encountering was a failure of empathy, a glitch in intersubjectivity. At this one moment in the text the writer had lapsed, relaxed, they had neglected to construct a robust model of the reader's mind inside their mind and consider how he might hold their sentence in contempt. Even if only for a second, the writer had loved themselves too much, and this self-love in the past had blown a black wind of hatred into the future, out of the writer's mind and into the reader. Grading his students' midterm papers, he'd made sure to mark every such blind spot in their sentences, teaching them to read themselves through his eyes, to read their sentences the way he read his own, which was how he imagined the smartest and best read and most hateful possible hypothetical reader would read them. Whenever a paper began *Since the dawn of time* or *Philosophy is comprised of...*, the reader underlined it and wrote *Cliché* or *Phrasing* in the margin, while thinking *My god* to himself, *Dumb, Moronic, Idiotic,* the reader thought, while he wrote *Word Choice?* or *-1* in the margin. His students had had unrestricted access to his mind—they listened to him lecture every day in class, they interrogated him during office hours—and even so they'd neglected to simulate for themselves what his mental experience of reading their first sentence might be like. The reader was determined never to make this mistake in his own prose. He strove to anticipate every hatred. In order to keep another reader from ever thinking *Moron* or *Impostor* tomorrow, he had to think *Moron* and *Impostor* tonight. The process might be painful in the present, but it would be a thousand times more painful for his future self to read the rejection. *Thank you for applying,* the letter's subtext would read, *but we regret to inform you that we hated you.* He let this hatred guide him toward the Fellowship. Every book he had managed to read in the past few weeks he had finished thanks to hatred. Quine. Ryle. Spinoza. It was research for his application, he told himself, research into how other readers reasoned. Maybe if you had read Quine, a voice inside his skull had said one night, you would be able to write this letter, and then, Maybe if you had read Spinoza. You've never even read Spinoza, he had thought, and then, But what about Ryle! Since he didn't know which books his readers might have read, the only rational strategy was to read everything. The goal, as with any syllabus, was synaptogenesis: by reading the books another reader has read, you can remake your brain in their brain's image. And so he'd passed one evening forcing Ryle through his eyeballs and into his head, the next evening forcing Spinoza into his head through his earholes (all physical copies of the *Ethics* had been checked out, but luckily the library had had one audiobook available). Whenever the reader couldn't write he read Ryle or listened to

Spinoza on 2x speed, instead of writing he fast-forwarded through a chipmunk-pitched Spinoza or skimmed Quine, confident that he would wake up the following morning fortified, a little bit smarter or at least a little less stupid, a bit better read, maybe tomorrow he would be able to vanquish the blankness of the document. The version of you who has read Spinoza can be the one to write the letter, he would reason, let him worry about it, not you, let *him* be the one the Fellowship judge judges, not you. In this way he had kept deferring the first sentence to a future self, who, he realized, he now suddenly was: tonight he had to be or become the smarter incarnation whose arrival he had been waiting for, for there wouldn't be any other. There was no tomorrow left to defer to, only the deadline. All his past selves' self-hatred had been preparing him for this moment, they had read so that he might write. Sitting in this carrel with a book each night, it had been torture to concentrate on the tiny type, but whenever his mind began to wander, the other minds would revive inside him, reviling him. It was enough to imagine a Quine scholar or a Ryle scholar reading his letter—*Fraud*, they said in his head, *Dilettante*—and he would sip his coffee and refocus. All he had to do was keep pouring black coffee over the waterwheel of his worthlessness, and as its paddles churned they propelled him forward, one page after another into his future. If nothing else, this was what he had learned from years of reading: the hydraulics of self-hatred. How to convert the waves of shame coursing through him into productive energy, so that his horror at not having read Heidegger could power him through the horror of reading Heidegger, could be the battery inside that boredom, keeping him going. There was no self-discipline or work ethic in the world, the reader knew, that could have motivated him in equal measure. That was the philosophy that had fueled his reading: not the love of wisdom, but the wisdom of hatred. His dissertation advisers had warned him that he would burn out this way, they were always encouraging him to take care of himself, take walks. But in the hour he would spend walking, the reader had calculated, he could read thirty pages. We just want to make sure you're happy in the program, his professors said, try to be compassionate with yourself. Compassionate? The reader had laughed grimly. Happy? He didn't want to be happy. The Fellowship judges wouldn't care whether he was happy. They wouldn't care whether he practiced *self-care*. All they would care about was whether he was smart enough. Speed-reading Foucault until two in the morning while refilling his Thermos with lukewarm coffee from the library's lobby's Starbucks station's pump-action carafe and ignoring the painful pounding in his temples might not make him happy, but *that's what would make him happy*. Whereas taking a walk would merely make him happy, which would throw him back into the deepest unhappiness, every happy step of the walk was in fact leading him ever nearer the abyss of being unhappy. If the reader was dumb and happy, the Fellowship would reject him, but if he was smart and miserable, they might accept him. That was the only advantage he had over the other applicants. He may not have studied with the most prestigious philosophers, he may not be writing his letter under the sign of N—, but unlike the others, he didn't need to be happy. He could withstand what for other readers would be hellish levels of self-hatred and self-negation. Let *them* be happy, let *them* practice self-care. Let *them* be compassionate toward themselves, and get rejected, the reader thought. He would be absolutely ruthless toward himself and get accepted. That was how he had made it this far, wasn't it? So why stop now, when he was only halfway there? Once he had arrived at the Fellowship, *then* he could take care of himself, or if not then, once he had found a job, or if not then, once he had published his own book, or if not then, once he was a real philosopher. He would relax when it was safe to relax, take a walk when it was safe. Until then he couldn't afford to ignore his hatred, in truth he feared he was nothing without it. Dear reader, the reader deleted, read dearer. He wondered what this year's judge would have read, when they were a Fellow. Then a brilliant idea occurred to him. Even if he didn't know who this year's judge would be, he could at least look up last year's Fellow. This was a profile page he hadn't studied closely yet, though it was a pattern he had observed in previous years: sometimes—in rare cases, when they were particularly accomplished—the most recent Fellow would be chosen to help select the next year's Fellow. He closed the letter and opened the Fellowship website, hovering the cursor over the Past Fellows link. Click it, a voice inside him commanded. At this thought the farthest track light clicked on across the room, spotlighting a row of bookshelves. The reader startled, but the row was empty. No one stood in the aisle of light. Hello? he called. The room remained deathly quiet, and after a few seconds the light clicked off again. He was alone here. It was as if his thought itself had triggered the light, he thought: as if the motion sensor had sensed, not the motion of another person, but the motion of his mind, the arrival of this other mind inside his mind. Click it, the voice commanded again. But he felt a powerful reluctance to click the link. Did he really want to know? Who last year's Fellow was? Or what they had read? Don't click it, he counseled himself. Close it. But by the time his mind had finished this thought his hand had clicked the link, was already scrolling down the page to last year's philosophy Fellow, who turned out to be a philosopher from N——. The reader had been rejected from N——. Judging by her dates she was the same age as him, they had probably both applied the same year. He read her profile carefully, her project description, the blood fled him as he read, his mind went gray. She had spent her Fellowship writing a book on Hegel's *Phenomenology of Spirit*. The reader had never read Hegel. He took another sip of coffee, but it had the same effect on his brain as spilling coffee on his laptop's track pad: the way that the cursor will begin to skid across the screen, driven by the phantom finger of the wetness's pressure, that was how his thoughts were spiraling now. She would be his reader, he was sure of it, he felt clairvoyant with dread. Why hadn't he read her profile sooner? While he had been customizing his consciousness for the hypothetical Ryle scholar, this actually existing Hegel scholar had been lying patiently in wait. *She* would be the one looking for any reason to reject him, *she* would be the reader stopping at his first mistake. Had it been a mistake to not read Hegel? What if she could tell? All it would take was one writer who was smarter than the reader, better read than the reader, one writer better acquainted with Hegel than the reader was, and if this applicant had so much as leafed through the *Phenomenology*—if their brain contained every book in the reader's brain plus one—then they would be accepted and he would be rejected, it really was that simple, he was in a struggle to the death for the recognition of the Fellow. All things being equal, the Fellow would award the Fellowship to the smarter writer. It's not as if the reader thought that a writer would have to namedrop Hegel, necessarily, making explicit references, in their letter, to the owl of Minerva, master and slave, the spirit is a bone. Even the reader could do that. He'd read Hegel's Wikipedia page. He'd read enough about or around Hegel to know how to invoke Hegel. The owl of Minerva flies at midnight, the reader had read somewhere, whatever that meant. If it were merely a matter of puffing up his letter with Hegelian philosophemes, the way a blowfish puffs out its cheeks, to intimidate his readers into thinking he had read Hegel—citation as deimatic display—then he could finish his letter in minutes. But while this kind of bluffing might carry him through his philosophy lectures, and impress his freshmen, it wouldn't be enough to fool the Fellow. She would be able to distinguish an impostor's letter from a real philosopher's letter. A writer who had read Hegel, it stood to reason, was bound to write slightly more confident, intelligent, convincing sentences than a writer who hadn't. The Fellow herself was proof of this. Some letters must just *feel* smarter than other letters, some people's minds must just look better on paper than other people's minds. Just as some people have more photogenic faces, some people must have more papyrogenic brains. This was the only knowledge that the reader had been trying to impart to his students, whenever he wrote *Cliché* or *Phrasing* on their papers. But he could see now that he had taught them nothing, all this time the blind had been leading the blind. With bitterness he remembered the student who had visited his office hours that very afternoon, his final meeting of the semester. The reader had been trying to read Ryle by winter light when he heard a timid knock at the door. It was a freshman whose name he couldn't even remember, a quiet pale presence who always slouched in the back row in a gray hoodie, glaring at his notebook with a gloomy intensity designed to repel the attention it invited, like a bonfire of shy-ness. He was standing in the office doorway, nervously declining the reader's offer of a seat and brandishing a bouquet of rolled-up pages in his hand. His midterm paper. The reader had returned them weeks ago. The freshman just had a few questions about his grade, he told the reader, before he had to turn in his final essay in class today. As the freshman flipped through the marked-up midterm page by page, pointing out each of the reader's marginalia and minus signs, asking what he had meant by *Phrasing*, why he had deducted so many points, the reader had kept casting trapped glances back at the copy of *The Concept of Mind* tented open on his desk. Every minute the freshman stood there was half a page of Ryle he had not read. He could feel his life dwindling away. *Ten points, ten points*, the freshman kept repeating, while the reader kept checking the time and thinking, *Ten pages, ten pages*. The freshman expected the reader to save him, at least to save his grade, but the reader could barely save himself, he needed to read. At last the freshman set the paper aside. The thing was, he told the reader, he was really enjoying this class, he'd even decided to study philosophy. *Since the dawn of time*, the paper's first sentence had read, *philosophy has been comprised of...* He just wanted to understand what he was doing wrong, the freshman said, what should he be doing instead, what did he need to do if one day he wanted to be like the reader? Was he even smart enough to become a real philosopher? Was he too stupid? He could take the truth. Be brutally honest. The freshman stared at him, radiating need for the reader's recognition, and the reader didn't know what to tell him. He must be mistaking him for someone else. He was standing there as solemnly as if he were in Socrates's office hours, but the reader wasn't Socrates, he wasn't even the Fellow, and at this rate he never would be. Idiot. Fuckup. The freshman must think that *this* is the end, the reader marveled, he must think that once he arrived at the reader's position—accepted to a philosophy program, granted an office to read books in and a class full of acolytes—he would have escaped the cycle of self-doubt, when in fact this was only the beginning, the freshman had no conception of the gulfs still separating this office from the Fellowship. Should he tell him? Professor? the freshman asked. Eventually the reader muttered a platitude about trying to read his final essay out loud, or backward, or backward out loud, his only other advice, he said, was to keep reading, to read everything, and try not to feel bad about a few points. The freshman thanked him and, thankfully, left, freeing the reader to read Ryle. But now, sitting in the carrel and staring out at the parking lot, where the snow had started to come down hard, he realized how pointless this advice had been. The freshman would never become the Fellow, following advice like that, and the odds were against him ever even becoming the reader. He should have told him the truth. It was too late for the reader, but maybe it wasn't too late for him. He was probably at a drunken dorm party tonight, celebrating the end of the semester and the submission of his final essay, but if he were here in the library, before him now, the reader would tell him the exact opposite of what he had: not to not feel bad, but precisely to *keep feeling bad*, to identify all the negative thoughts he was feeling about himself when he saw those negative points on his paper and to harness them, to be prepared to tarry with the negative for years, because this was what he was studying philosophy to learn, to understand that there existed other minds in the world who hated him, that not everyone loved him the way his parents or high school teachers or guidance counselors had loved him, that the reader's own way of loving him was to hate him, to become the hateful voice inside him, passing the hatred onto him, transferring all the other minds he'd ever accumulated inside his mind into the freshman's mind, this was what *Phrasing* had meant and what all teaching should be, the goal, as with any line edits, was synaptogenesis, to remake the freshman's brain in his brain's image, indeed, the reader would tell him, if he *really* wanted to know the truth, if he wanted the reader to be *brutally honest* and teach him what the reader thought it was important for him to know— this was the only lesson the reader wished his own professors had taught him before it was too late, before he had graduated and applied everywhere (to N——, for travel grants, to journals), only to be rejected from them all, rejected not just unanimously but etymologically, literally thrown (*jacere*) back (*re-*) here, to the same philosophical backwater he'd attended as a freshman himself years ago, which was the only program to accept him, and which had never, as far as the reader knew, sent anyone to N——, much less to the Fellowship—then he wouldn't have written *Phrasing* on the freshman's paper at all, he would have written *Fuckup* or *Idiot* in the margin, because at least then he would appreciate how much hatred was at stake. There was still time for the freshman to escape this cycle, to study anything else, but if he was as determined as he claimed to become a real philosopher, then that was what he was going to need to understand. As long as he learned to obey this voice early, the reader should have told him, he could not only become but might even overtake the reader. If he read Hegel now, he should have told him—if he didn't wait even another day to read Hegel—he could make it further than the reader had made it. The reader ground his palm savagely into his forehead. Fuckhead. Failure. Fraud. He was already a decade older than the freshman, the same age as the Fellow, and still he hadn't read Hegel. What had he been waiting for? He had read Arendt, Benjamin, and Cavell, but never Hegel. Descartes yes, but Hegel no. He chewed his nail, his cheek. Reject. Reject. Eckhart, Fanon, and Guattari, but not the *Phenomenology*. Somehow he had read Heidegger, Irigaray, and Jameson before Hegel. While the Fellow had been reading Hegel, what had he even been reading? Kant, Lacan, Mainländer. Nietzsche, Ortega y Gasset, Pascal. Oh god. Night after night in the library he had been forcing Quine, Ryle, and Spinoza into his head, when what he could and should have been—when what nothing had been stopping him from—reading was Hegel. It would have been so easy to read Hegel. His library if not his life flashed before his eyes, all the books he had read instead of the *Phenomenology*. Toufic, von Uexküll, Voltaire. Wittgenstein, Xenophon, Yourcenar. Would the Fellow care that he had read Zupančič, if he'd never read Hegel? She'd probably read Hegel in short pants. As a child the reader had read every volume of R.L. Stine's *Goosebumps*, he winced to remember all those nights he had wasted under his blanket with a flashlight, staying up late to finish *The Scarecrow Walks At Midnight* or *Say Cheese and Die!*, when even then he could have been starting the *Phenomenology*. How did it happen—but this was how it always happens—how had that led to this? The scarecrow of Minerva walks at midnight. How had he gone from *Goosebumps* to graduate school, how had he ended up in this carrel? His head was throbbing. He looked out the window, surveilling the miniature students crawling across the parking lot, and he had the fleeting autoscopic impression that each was him, that he was watching himself head home from class in the past. He could see it clearly now: because he had loved reading as a child he had done well in literature courses and on tests, placing into his high school's honors track, where gradually he had learned to read more difficult books, to submit himself to that difficulty, to become a cenobite of boredom, until soon he was scoring even higher on even harder tests, and because of all this—the As on the report cards, the perfect verbals—he'd been awarded a scholarship here, which must mean, he had thought naively at the time, that he was good at reading, that if he went on reading more books—the hardest, most difficult books, the ones that even other readers didn't read—he might have a future as a reader. He would keep being rewarded, he'd imagined, lifted upward, he would be allowed to go on reading, *as long as he kept reading.* It wasn't until he'd been rejected that he'd learned the truth: that this whole time there had been other readers out there in the world, readers like the Fellow, who had known or been told to read even better books, or simply more of them, they were the ones who would be allowed to become real readers. He'd been trying to catch up with them ever since, and still he hadn't read enough, nothing was ever enough, only everything would be enough. He thought he'd been obeying his self-hatred, but even he had loved himself too much, that much was becoming clear. He closed the browser and reopened the letter. He typed the Fellow's name, deleted it. He drank from his Thermos until sweat beaded on his scalp like condensation— drops of brain escaping—then ran a hand through his hair to smush them back in. Finally he googled the Fellow. It didn't take long to find her profile on N—'s People page. She had returned there after the Fellowship, this time as a real philosopher, and her Hegel book, he saw, was forthcoming next year. Her photo showed her smiling in front of a set of built-in bookshelves painted white. The reader spent the next fifteen minutes in the library slowly zooming in on her library, magnifying the low-resolution background to try to make out the blurred titles on the spines. He assumed Brandom was in there somewhere, Butler, along with Inwood and Kojève and every other book he'd ever been meaning to read, but he couldn't decipher the text and didn't recognize the jacket designs. Giving up, he zoomed back out to the Fellow's smiling face. Except that now, strangely, her smile read more like a smirk. There was a contempt in her expression that he hadn't noticed there before. He knew this was an illusion—it had to be the same smile, the contempt was Kuleshovian—but still he felt rejected by this face. Idiot, the face said. Impostor. Hegel Hegel Hegel, the face said. He searched the Fellow's name on Twitter. After a few false positives—a think tank analyst, a podcaster—he located her account. He could tell it was hers because she had the Fellowship in her bio, followed by the 🌐 emoji beside the word *Spirit*. The first thing he did was search her posts for *Hegel*. He found a thread where she and other philosophers were trading Hegel puns. *ALFhebung*, the Fellow posted, with a photo of the armadillo-nosed sitcom alien posing with a rose in his mouth. *The virgin Hegel versus the chad Schopenhauer*, another philosopher posted, with Schopenhauer's head photoshopped onto a bodybuilder's body, while Hegel's head was photoshopped onto a scrawny teenager's body, to which the Fellow responded, *The virgin Schopenhauer versus the chad Hegel*, with the heads swapped. *Poppyseed Hegel*, another philosopher posted, *is that something?*, and the Fellow posted, *The* ▩ *spirit* ▩ *is* ▩ *a* ▩ *boner* ▩. The reader smiled tightly. So. This was the mind who would be reading him. This was the mind he had to model inside his mind. Forget the *comprised of* hater, the *seminal* hater, forget the Quine scholar and the Spinoza scholar. He googled her again, scrolled down until he found her LinkedIn profile, clicked it without blinking. Yes, he thought, now we were cooking with gas. How would someone who had gone straight from N— to the Fellowship, someone who before that had worked as an editorial assistant at the *Phenomenological Quarterly* (the reader had been rejected from the *Phenomenological Quarterly*) and before that had received a travel grant to Berlin (the reader had been rejected for the same travel grant, the same year), someone who had made a pilgrimage and posed, he saw when he zoomed in on her profile photo, beside Hegel's headstone at Dorotheenstadt cemetery, someone therefore who had not only read Hegel, leafed through Hegel, but who had devoted her life (a life that it was dawning on the reader with drymouth horror, as he doomscrolled down her vita, was the mirror image of his own, accepted precisely where he had been rejected, advanced forward exactly when he had been thrown back, for no reason that he could discern other than that she had read Hegel and he had not), in short someone who had devoted her entire life to Hegel, how would such a reader read his letter? All his life, if someone had asked him why he read, the reader would have told them that he was curious about *other minds*. He read philosophy, he would have told them, to learn how other minds saw the world. But now the only mind in the world that mattered was the Fellow's. What the reader needed to know was how one mind in particular saw, not the world, but his letter. He didn't need to read Hegel to learn how Hegel saw the world but to learn how *someone who had read Hegel would see his letter.* You're wasting your time writing this letter, he imagined the Fellow would tell him. How do you expect to write the first sentence of your letter, if you still haven't read the first word of Hegel? She was right. She was absolutely right. If he had read the *Phenomenology* earlier, he might have been the one to go to N—, the *Phenomenological Quarterly*, Berlin. Maybe there was still time to make it to the Fellowship. The reader paced to the library's catalogue computer against the far wall. With each row of bookshelves that he passed through, the track lights clicked on above him, he strode into the darkness trailing a wake of weak fluorescence. The catalogue showed a single copy of the *Phenomenology* available, one floor below. There were still two hours before the library closed. If he got Hegel now, he might be able to read sixty pages by the end of the night. But that was suicidal, he knew. He couldn't waste a single minute reading Hegel. The application was due tomorrow, and he still had essays to grade. Nothing could be more dangerous than ignoring his letter. Except wouldn't the truly dangerous thing, the Fellow reasoned inside him, be to ignore his self-hatred? It wasn't any different from ignoring pain. Hate, like heat, was just afferent information that your body needed to share with your mind. It was a way of alerting you to some danger out there in the world. If the letter was hot with hate, it was this voice inside you's way of warning you: try to write tonight and you'll get burned. Would you keep your hand pressed to a hot stovetop? Would you ignore a smarting finger? Then why ignore this warning that you still aren't smart enough? Self-hatred is just a fingertip for touching the future with. A nerve inside of time. The ghostly thread of it binds today's brain to tomorrow's brain—it can feel out tomorrow's worst-case scenarios today—and tonight it's telling you that you need to read Hegel. It's clear you aren't getting any writing done anyway, the Fellow reasoned. In the hour you've been sitting here you could have read thirty pages. If you get the *Phenomenology* you'll go to sleep with the bare minimum of Hegel in your head, and at least that will be better than nothing: the worst first sentence you could write in the morning would still be better than the best first sentence you could write tonight. Whereas if you stay at your laptop, you'll only be postponing the inevitable: tomorrow you'll wake in bed with the same brain you went to sleep with, and you'll wind up stuck in the same place in the same blank document. Impostor, you'll think all over again. Fraud. Then won't you just have to spend *tomorrow* reading Hegel? Wouldn't you merely have deferred the *Phenomenology* for your future self to read? Where else do you think the hatred even comes from? It's not self-hatred, it's your future self's hatred. Your future self hates you for not reading Hegel, because it means that he's the one who has to read Hegel. *He's* the one who thinks you're an idiot, who resents your procrastination for sabotaging him, he's the one whose hatred has been echoing backward from tomorrow to haunt you. If you don't read Hegel now, tomorrow you will be the voice that has been hating you tonight, just as yesterday you were hearing tonight's hatred— hauntred—in your head. All right, the reader thought, all right, you're right. He hurried down the empty stairwell, his steps casting cavernous echoes. He could grade papers in the morning, he thought, there would still be time. He had all afternoon to write the letter. Tonight he just had to find Hegel. When he arrived at the lower floor, it was equally deserted as upstairs, the stacks all dark but one. At the end of the room a single track light glowed above a row of bookshelves, spotlighting them like a god shaft after a storm. The reader knew without needing to check that this was where he would find Hegel. It was a sign. He paced down the aisles, triggering the track lights as he moved, dispersing the darkness with every step. When he reached the final haloed row, it was labeled Gu-Ho. Yes, he thought, a sign. It was only as he was striding past the books themselves, scanning the library stickers for the *Phenomenology*'s call number, that a nauseating certainty rose in him. Because why had this aisle been lit in the first place? He hadn't seen anyone else in the room with him. Fear placed one foot in front of the other. He inspected every shelf, and it was just as he dreaded: the *Phenomenology* had gone missing. Right where it should be—between the *Lectures on Aesthetics* and the *Science of Logic*—there was a fat gap. How was it possible? The catalogue had listed it as available, just minutes ago. It doesn't matter, the Fellow said. The judges won't care what your excuse is, all they'll care about is the fact that you haven't read Hegel. I know, the reader thought, I *know* that. Thank you for applying, the Fellow said. We regret to inform you. The reader swept the room, starting from the back and checking every carrel desktop, every pile of books, every book cart. The *Phenomenology* had to be here somewhere, he told himself, it couldn't have gotten far. But deep down he knew it was gone. Maybe he could get by with skimming Kojève, he thought, and there was a burst of bitter laughter in his skull. LOL, the Fellow said. Do you think I got where I am by skimming Kojève? Okay, the reader thought, pounding his temple with his palm, like a swimmer struggling to unplug an ear. We've got a Hegel expert here, the Fellow said. Guy's skimmed Kojève.

He's even read Hegel's Wikipedia page! All right, all right, the reader pounded, as he rounded the last row of shelves, I'll read it, I'll read the *Phenomenology*. It was then that he saw him: across the room, in a carrel in the far corner, with his back to the reader but still recognizable—unmistakable—by his gray hoodie and scoliotic slouch, slumped the freshman. His head was buried in what looked like a phonebook. He must have felt the reader's gaze on the nape of his neck—a prey phenomenon that some ethologists called the *holy shiver*, the reader had read somewhere—because he turned around just then, meeting the reader's eyes. Oh, the freshman called out. Hi, Professor. The reader waved feebly as he approached the carrel and leaned over the book, trying to spy the title. The freshman flashed the cover—G.W.F. Hegel's *Phenomenology of Spirit*—while marking his place with a finger. By the looks of it he had read about thirty pages. The freshman brushed his hair and his hood out of his eyes and thanked the reader for meeting with him in his office earlier. He'd decided to take his advice, he said, starting tonight. His advice? The reader cast his mind back in panic. What had he told him? Read books, he had said then, read everything. But *why* had he said that? What had he been thinking? He hadn't been thinking, he had been digging his own grave without knowing it, and now he had his past self to thank for this pit he was standing in. Idiot, he thought, Fuckup, trying to beam this thought backward eight hours in time, into his head in his office this afternoon. Even so, he couldn't help smiling. It had turned out to be good advice, despite everything. Maybe the freshman would make it far after all: *he* would go to N—, and then Berlin, *he* would enter the Fellowship and emerge from it, in all things the freshman would become the Fellow. That was great, the

reader told him. That was very admirable. But, he explained—
and this was as awkward for him as it was for the freshman—he
actually needed that book. Would he mind letting him have it?
The freshman hesitated. Weren't there other copies, he asked.
The reader shook his head. It was urgent, he said, an emergency.
Normally he would just buy it, he lied—in fact he could never
afford it, he had already spent his stipend on food—but he
needed the book tonight, for very important research. The
freshman frowned at the *Phenomenology*, as though it were his
wallet and the reader were a beggar in the street. He's considering it, the reader realized, with a beggar's telepathy. Take it, the
Fellow said. Take it now! Just threaten to fail him and
take the book. The reader tried reasoning with the freshman one
last time. You don't even need to read it yet, he reassured him,
not for many years, not until after you've read Aristotle and
Kant and Fichte. In the middle of the sentence he could tell it
was the wrong sentence, but the words had left his mouth, there
was no deleting them. The freshman stiffened, unconvinced. It
was obvious that he *did* need to read it, the reader's desperation
to read it showed him plainly what a future of not having read it
looked like. By the pity in his eyes, he could see that the freshman could see him clearly now: he was no Socrates, just some
thrown-back backwater adjunct and specter of rejection, a hun-
gry ghost doomed to haunt the stacks and steal books from the
living, which was what the freshman risked becoming, if he
handed over Hegel. The reader waved off this vision, dismissing
not just the book but the entire situation. Never mind, he told
the freshman. Forget about it. He should keep it: the reader
could always find a copy online. Thanks, Professor, the freshman said uncertainly, and neither of them knew what he was

thanking him for. The reader left him there. Halfway to the stairwell he heard the freshman call out, I hope you enjoy my essay, and without turning back he raised his hand in parting. Oh, he was going to enjoy his essay all right, he was going to make him pay for Hegel with every typo. Hegel Hegel Hegel, he thought as he climbed the stairs, to shove down the last few minutes into oblivion, to keep from remembering a single thing that had just happened, Hegel Hegel Hegel. Once he was upstairs, out of earshot, he jogged to his carrel, taking a zigzag path through the stacks to trigger every track light. He'd lost only five minutes, he calculated, two pages. There was still time. Back at his laptop he googled the *Phenomenology*. Scrolling through an out-of-copyright translation on archive.org, he clicked the link to the Preface and tried to read Hegel's first sentence. You should be writing right now, he thought, as his eyes scanned from left to right. As his eyes moved up and down, he thought, The deadline is tomorrow. Before he knew it he had somehow reached the bottom of the page, and he couldn't remember a single word he had just read. He *hadn't* read a single word, because he had retained nothing. His eyes had failed to transport even one sentence off the screen and into his mind. He started from the top again, but when he reached the bottom it was the same. He remembered nothing. Focus, the Fellow said. He sipped from his Thermos. Hegel Hegel Hegel. He read the page a third time, but even as his eyes passed over Hegel's words, the only words passing through his mind were *Reject, Failure*, it was as if these were the only words actually printed there, over and over, as though someone had replaced the text of the *Phenomenology* with this lorem ipsum of loathing. He assumed the freshman was having better luck downstairs, he'd probably already read another thirty pages. When he saw that half an hour had gone by he gave up, closing Hegel and reopening the letter. The cursor was still blinking where he'd left it. A face glared back at him from within the blackness of the blank screen. Raising his hand to his temple, he saw the face touch itself as well, and there was a contempt in the reflection that he hadn't noticed there before. Idiot, the face said. Impostor. The Fellow was right, the reader thought. This could be his future self he was seeing. Whenever he thought dark thoughts, this must be the dark face that uttered them. The other self inside him—the self that lay hidden on the shadow side of his mind, the shadow side of the hyphen, the secret subject behind all his self-consciousness, self-doubt, self-pity—was regarding him from tomorrow here. And he could see that tomorrow would be the same as today. He would wake in bed with the same Hegel-less brain. He would grade his students' papers and return to this carrel. And whether he wrote the letter or not—whether he was accepted to the Fellowship or rejected, whether he stayed in this program and finished his dissertation or whether he left altogether—he would always be the one who had to read what he had not read. After Hegel there would be Brandom, then Butler, and after Butler, Inwood, or Kojève, and then (how could he have forgotten?) the Fellow herself, whose own book would be added to this archive soon enough, added to the bad infinity of this bottomless bibliography. You still haven't read the Fellow, a voice would be hissing inside his head one year from now, either in the Fellowship's library or this one, it would make no difference. He closed the letter without saving his changes—there were no changes to save—and stared out the window. It was late now, past midnight, and in the empty parking lot he spotted a sole hooded figure, loping against the snow. He was fairly sure it was the freshman. The way he slouched even while walking, scarecrow of Minerva. One arm hung at his side, and he seemed to be holding something in his hand. The reader tried to make out whether it was a book, whether the freshman was taking Hegel home with him. He was too far off to be certain, it could be either the *Phenomenology* or his phone. He watched the figure dwindle down the street, and when he had disappeared in the darkness, the reader withdrew the stack of essays from his backpack, flipping through them until he had found the freshman's. Webster's *defines 'philosophy,'* the first sentence read, *as the love of wisdom*. My god, the reader thought, as he uncapped his pen and underlined the first sentence. Cliché, he thought. Idiotic. But when he brought his pen to the margin, he did not write *Cliché* or *Idiotic*. He didn't even write *Phrasing*. He thought of the freshman sitting in the carrel downstairs, forcing Hegel into his head through his eyeballs, wondering whether he would ever be smart enough. He thought of him walking home through the cold, gripping the *Phenomenology* in freezing fingers, counting down the pages he could be reading with each passing step. He imagined what it would be like— inside the freshman's mind—when he got this final essay back and read over the reader's notes. And for the first time he could understand what his professors had been trying to tell him. Two tomorrows unfolded inside him. If he wrote *Cliché* or *Phrasing* now, he saw, the freshman might learn to hate himself, and maybe that would spare him a rejection, in the end. But the reader could choose to spare him the hatred altogether. He might not be able to help him become the Fellow, but at least he could steer him away from becoming the reader, he could practice that compassion toward the freshman that he could not practice toward himself. Even if it wasn't much, it still might be enough: the other minds might stay confined inside his mind, the freshman might go the rest of his life without ever needing to know about them. Dumb and happy! Dumb and happy... The reader wrote *Good* and made a check mark in the margin, then flipped to the last page and wrote *A*+. He put the essay away and regarded his reflection in the deadened laptop glass. Yes. He could see it clearly now: his future, the freshman's, the Fellow's. Dear readers. After a minute the first of the track lights clicked off across the room, and darkness showered down on the farthest row of shelves. The next track light deactivated half a second afterward, and then the next, so that the darkness came staggered, clicking closer to the carrel with every row. This wall of shadow advanced across the stacks like an avalanche, soon it would consume him. At any moment, the reader knew, he could stop it. All he had to do was raise his hand. But he just kept still and watched it. He waited for the black wind blowing over the books to blow over him also.

A NIGHTMARE

BEHIND THE ABANDONED HOUSE I DISCOVERED A
grassy field. Stretched across the length of the field was a row
of shopping carts. They were not nested inside one another,
as they would be in the corral of a parking lot. Instead they
had been welded end to end. Their front and rear panels had
been removed, and their sides had been fused together, so that
their wireframe floors paved an uninterrupted pathway across
the field, an elevated metallic catwalk leading to the forest at
the field's edge. It was dusk. The sky was tangerine. Above
the forest, a blood-blister sun was hovering over the inky line
of trees. Aside from the abandoned house, the only sign of
human habitation in sight was this corridor of shopping carts.
The monumentality of the design, combined with the enigma
of its purpose, lent the structure a sense of ancientness and
alterity. It evoked a distant civilization, whose rituals and sym-
bolic orders were unknowable to me: as if it were a ruin that
had been rusting in this field for thousands of years, enduring
sun, rain, snow, and slow centuries, waiting for the day when
some archaeologist would step into the clearing and uncover
it. Even though I knew that this was impossible—even though
I recognized, in my rational mind, my waking or my daylight
mind, that the shopping carts had to have been gathered from
a grocery store this century—I could not shake the impression of a far architect, or fathom any contemporary consciousness that could have constructed this. The monument had to
have hailed from another time, or another place, for another

151

purpose. Even if the materials were new, I thought, the design itself must be ancient or alien: whoever made this must have been working from an obscure blueprint, substituting shopping carts for whatever materials or technologies had been originally called for. I approached the first cart, the threshold of the corridor. Its floor was level with my waist, and I leaned against the cool metal. Staring down the long line of carts—their sidewalls guided my gaze toward the green vanishing point of the forest at their end—I felt as if I were peering into an abyss. The distance seemed steep, vertical, and the same dizziness gripped me as when I look down from a high balcony. That ledge-drunk urge to step over every precipice. I had to resist the temptation to climb onto the shopping cart and let myself—this was the word that came to me—plummet. If I set foot on the cart, I understood, I would be sucked into the forest in an instant. And it occurred to me that this could be the only purpose of the corridor, its original design: to draw people from one end to the other, from the house to the woods. This corridor had been engineered to direct the flow of human bodies, just as aqueducts were designed to channel water. I could picture it now. Linked together, what the shopping carts formed was a long metallic straw, for siphoning the libations or sacrifices that were offered to it. And at the end of this straw? Whatever is at the end of all straws, sucking. I squinted into the distance, where the farthest carts glinted in the sunset, disappearing into the forest. There was no way of telling how far they extended beyond the tree line. Maybe miles. It was possible that the corridor led straight through the woods and that then, emerging on the other side, it divaricated into an immense maze, the shopping carts branching out in gray angles and radiating chambers across a vast plain, coiling as tightly as intestines around a single point at their center. Cautiously, I climbed onto the first cart. Its sidewalls rose to my thighs. The wire flooring was strong, unyielding beneath my weight, and the structure was unexpectedly stable. The cart did not budge or roll, and I realized that the casters must have been removed. A breeze blew toward me from the end of the corridor, seeming to originate from deep within the forest. I stepped forward, advancing from the first shopping cart to the second, then to the third. I kept walking like this for minutes, though no matter how long I walked, the forest never seemed to grow any closer. The trees remained the same size, at seemingly the same distance, as if I were merely walking in place, on a treadmill of metal. Eventually I began to jog, and the rattling of the carts grew loud, as shrill as cicadas' chirring. Still the forest seemed fixed. I pushed myself to run faster, racing to reach the end of the corridor, to reach it before—but before what, I could not say. When I asked myself what it was I thought I was racing against, the only explanation I could summon was the sunset. The sinking sun had turned the air of the field bloodred, and I sensed that there were only minutes of daylight left. Soon the field would be plunged in darkness. And no matter what, I did not want to be caught in the shopping carts when darkness fell. I did not know what I thought would happen then, only that I could not risk it. Whatever it was, this machine had been built for darkness. I could sense this. The whole thing would hum to life at nightfall. While the sun was still visible, I had to reach the end of the corridor, with enough time to turn around and run back, and I had to be sure that my feet were on solid earth before the first shadows filled the trough of the shopping carts. Even as I thought this, the sun sank below the trees, and the sky darkened. Everything became black as during a storm. I could barely see the silver flooring beneath my feet. I'm disappearing, I thought, crazily. I'm disappearing. Then the air was lit from behind with a crimson tint, as if by a stoplight in fog. When I turned back I saw, rising over the roof of the abandoned house, a blood moon. No sooner had the sun set in the west than this moon had risen in the east, drenching the field and the shopping carts in its red light. Though the moon filled me with dread, I was relieved to see how close I still was to the house. In all the time I had been running I had managed to cover only half the field. I returned to the house now, ignoring the forest behind me. Hurrying toward the corridor's entrance, I kept my eyes fixed on the first cart, impatient to leap from its edge to the safety of the grass. As long as I did not turn around, I thought, as long as I did not look back, I might still be saved. Otherwise it was too late. The sun had set. Darkness had fallen. The moon had risen. And at the end of the corridor behind me, somewhere beyond the forest, at the center of the gray maze that the shopping carts made, a mouth would be opening. At that very moment, as if in response to this thought, there came from within the house a howling sound like a tornado siren: the terrified baying of bloodhounds.

THE POSTCARD

THE CLIENT TURNED OUT TO BE AN OLDER MAN, A
lawyer nearing retirement.

I met him at his office downtown, where he gestured for me
to sit across the desk from him, as though I were the client and
his were the services we were there to discuss.

After introducing himself he produced a manila envelope
from a drawer and withdrew a postcard.

The postcard showed an aerial photograph of a seaside highway: a two-lane road hugged a steep cliff, thickly forested with
pine trees; on the shoreline below a gray sea stretched flat and
featureless from a rocky strand.

In the distance there was a dark bank of clouds, presaging
storm.

Heavy white fog clung to the tops of the pine trees, creeped
along the beach.

Printed at the top of the postcard, in the sunny yellow cursive and blocky font of a tourism bureau, utterly at odds with
the bleakness of the tableau, were the words *Meet Me In Ocean
View!*

I gathered that Ocean View was the name of a resort town
along this highway, though there were no road signs visible, and
it was impossible to tell, from the photo alone, which direction
along the highway Ocean View was likeliest to lie in.

There was not only no town pictured in the photograph, but no visible person to meet there either: no smiling tourist, no car on the highway, not even a motel in the distance, in short no trace of human life.

Only a deserted highway along a cold beach.

Turn it over, the client said.

I placed the postcard face down on the desk and saw that there was a handwritten message inked neatly on the back.

Ocean View Motel, Room 315, S.H.

It was postmarked last week, at Ocean View's post office.

My wife and I visited Ocean View on our honeymoon, five decades ago now, the client explained.

They had stayed for a weekend at the Ocean View Motel.

When I did not respond he added, In room 315.

S.H. were, of course, his wife's initials.

I asked him whether he believed his wife had sent him this postcard.

He shook his head.

My wife is dead, he said.

His wife had died last year, he clarified, exactly one year to the day that the postcard had arrived.

He went on to describe some of the symptoms of what he referred to only as her *memory disease.*

Circular conversations, repetition, misrecognition, disorientation.

Strange loops.

160

I asked whether they had ever returned to the town or to the motel, either together or alone, perhaps for a vacation or an anniversary.

No, he said, without elaborating.

He handed me a faded photograph.

The photograph featured a young man—recognizably the client, years ago, back when he had been close, I estimated, to my own age—posing with a young woman beside the motel's road sign.

They had apparently just arrived, the evidence of a long drive—suitcases, groceries—visible in the car behind them.

In the background I could see the motel, a squat block of orange stucco, with turquoise trim.

From the envelope, the client now produced a silver room key, attached to a green plastic tag in the shape of a diamond.

Embossed in white was the room number: 315.

A memento, he said, we kept the spare.

He pushed the key across the table.

Keep it, he told me, take it with you, it may prove useful.

I asked what he wanted me to do.

Go to Ocean View—the motel still exists, he said, after all these years—and see who is staying there, who sent this postcard, and why, see who, if anyone, is renting room 315, what they want from me.

He had tried calling, but no one answered.

I told him that it was probably a prank and asked whether there was anyone he could think of who would wish him ill, anyone with enough knowledge of his marriage and their honeymoon to have sent this postcard, anyone his wife might have told about Ocean View, for instance any children or lovers, I suggested.

He shook his head.

I've thought of all that, he said, there's no one she could have told, even she would have forgotten the honeymoon in the end.

She had spent her last years in a mental fog, he explained, in a facility, on bad days she barely recognized him, even after he reminded her of who he was she would forget.

He stared out his office window.

Every few minutes, he went on, she would look back at him brightly, as if he had just walked into the room, asking who he was, what he was doing there, as if they hadn't been talking the entire time, every instant she saw him was like the first time she had ever seen him.

The last time he visited she had been with another man in the facility, a fellow resident, whom she had introduced to him as her husband: Thank you for visiting, she had told him, I want you to meet my husband, before gesturing to the blankly smiling stranger beside her.

After this he could not bear to see her, it had been a year since he had visited or even called by the time she died.

So you see, he concluded, she would never have been able to recall the name of the town, much less the motel, much less the room number.

I asked him what else he remembered from their honeymoon, anywhere they might have gone in town, no matter how insignificant, any detail might be helpful to me.

He thought a moment and said they did take a tour of some kind of factory there, he could no longer recall what or where exactly, just the dim memory of iron machinery, vast rooms, a slow afternoon listening to the droning of a docent.

He had not thought of that afternoon in years, he said, not until I had asked.

He pushed his business card across the desk, with his private number on it.

He would pay my daily rate plus expenses, he told me, for as long as it took.

Let me know as soon as you find anything, he said.

I flew to the nearest airport, in the town of N—, little more than a landing strip in the woods, and rented a car there, an anonymous black sedan.

Ocean View was half a day's drive.

I entered the motel's address in the GPS and listened to the cool robotic voice as it guided me toward my destination.

Proceed to the route, it commanded.

You will arrive at... Ocean View Motel... in five hours and fifteen minutes.

I called my client once from the road, but he did not answer.

Otherwise I drove in silence, the hours melting past in a trance broken only by the intermittent instructions of the GPS device, which commanded me in an unvarying second-person address, the mood of hypnotic suggestion, of mesmerism.

Turn right, merge left, you will arrive.

I thought of my client visiting his wife in the facility, trying to communicate with her in this same calm, compassionate monotone, commanding her to remember.

You are my wife, I am your husband.

Guiding her into the present.

The route that the device had chosen for me followed a single scenic highway for several hundred miles, a curving two-lane road that wound along the ocean on my right.

I kept glancing out the window expectantly, waiting to recognize the stretch of coastline from the postcard.

Soon, I thought, I would enter the image.

And then, without my noticing when it had happened, the landscape had become familiar to me.

To my right I saw the bleak beach of gray rocks, a dark bank of clouds far out over the water, and for a moment I had the distinct impression that I had been there before.

It was the same strand from the postcard.

I had crossed over that border that separates what is familiar from what is strange, I had trespassed into the terrain or the district of déjà vu.

The beach was just as deserted in reality as in the photograph, and just as foggy too.

At some point thick white wisps had begun to billow over my windshield, and the closer I drew to Ocean View, the denser the fog became.

I even had to turn on my high-beams, though it was the middle of the day.

The headlights penetrated only a few feet in front of me, and I could see ahead by just a single lane divider at a time.

One yellow line after another blurred beneath the hood of my car.

No sooner had one line vanished into the fog behind me than another materialized from out of the fog before me, yellow link following yellow link, I thought, in a chain of instants.

Welcome to Ocean View, a passing billboard flashed, before sinking into the mist in my rearview mirror.

The destination is on your left, the robotic voice announced.

I slowed in time to see the dim outline of the Ocean View Motel, just visible through the fog roiling against my passenger window.

I pulled into the lot, parked near the entrance.

Mine was the only car in sight.

Were it not for the wan light in the windows of the lobby, I would have assumed that the motel had long gone out of business.

You have arrived, the voice announced.

I checked my client's photograph to compare.

Like the beach, the building was identical to its image.

Nothing had changed in the intervening decades, not the orange paint of the stucco nor the turquoise trim, it was a structure untouched by time.

Even the roadside sign appeared to be the same: instead of a light box atop a tall metal highway pole—ubiquitous among modern hotel chains—there was the same modest wooden vintage billboard that my client and his wife had posed beside in his photograph, still staked into the grass of the road verge, with the words *Ocean View* freshly painted in turquoise cursive.

The building stood exactly as my client would have remembered it.

If he had been the one to return here, it no doubt would have felt like reentering a memory.

And perhaps, it occurred to me, that was why he had sent me in his place.

I had not thought to wonder before that moment why he had hired me, rather than coming here himself.

I had assumed he feared some danger waiting for him on the other side of the postcard, blackmail or a trap, but perhaps he simply preferred not to revisit or remember Ocean View, now that his wife was gone, he had not specified, after all, whether his memory of the honeymoon was a happy one, nor for that matter his memory of his marriage.

These were the kinds of questions I was paid not to ask, it was safest to assume that my clients were unhappy—adulterers, stalkers, divorcers—if you hired me at all it was because you belonged to the race of the betrayers and the betrayed.

When I entered the lobby there was no one at the front desk.

I rang the silver bell on the counter and waited for what felt like several minutes before crossing the lobby to investigate a wire rack of postcards in the corner.

There was the same *Meet Me In Ocean View!* postcard that my client had received, as well as a postcard featuring white sails luffing across the foggy water, and—this was the image

I lingered over—a postcard featuring a strange brick building, immense and narrowly windowed, fronted by an iron gate and flanked by what seemed to be two large smokestacks.

This must be the factory my client had visited, a relic—I found myself imagining—of Ocean View's industrial past, not photogenic as architecture but somehow historically significant, possibly a museum now.

As for what the factory might have produced, I could not imagine, maybe its twin smokestacks manufactured all of Ocean View's fog.

May I help you, a voice called.

At the front desk an older woman had appeared, probably the same age as my client and his wife, she could even have been working here the weekend that they came, all those years ago, perhaps she was the one who had taken their photo.

I told her I would like to book a room for the weekend.

She asked whether I preferred smoking or nonsmoking, and I replied that my only preference was that I stay in room 315.

She regarded me then for the first time—the request had surprised her—but she did not question me.

I'm sorry, she said, that room is occupied.

She asked, again, whether I would prefer smoking or nonsmoking.

I told her my only preference was to stay on the third floor, and that if 315 was unavailable, then 313 would suffice.

Then I thought to ask whether 315 might be available soon.

I had prepared a story if she asked—that it had been the site of my honeymoon, a source of fond memories, nostalgia—but she did not ask.

She regarded me again and simply told me no, she did not know when the current occupant planned to check out.

I thanked her and said that in that case I would be happy to take 313.

She smiled for the first time—as though suddenly remembering our roles as clerk and customer—and asked whether I took a smoking or nonsmoking room.

Either is fine, I reminded her, whatever 313 happened to be.

That's right, she said apologetically, you told me that already.

313 was nonsmoking, she explained, but I could smoke in the parking lot out back.

She gave me a contract to fill out, and when I reached the signature line I hesitated at the thought of signing my client's name.

I always assumed my clients' names.

But I remembered the blankly smiling man my client had told me about, the fellow resident whom S.H. had introduced to him as himself—meet my husband, she had told him—the last time he had visited her.

This stranger, too, had assumed his name, or at least his identity, and how many of us could fit, I wondered, inside one man's name, before I signed that name on the dotted line and handed the contract back to the woman.

She looked at it a moment, suspiciously I thought, then put it away, presenting me with a white plastic keycard for my room.

She noted my surprise at the card—I had been expecting a vintage silver key like my client's, I still had it in my pocket—and she asked whether I had any other questions.

I produced my client's postcard from my suitcase and slid it across the desk.

I explained that a friend had mailed it to me, did she remember selling it to anyone in recent weeks?

She frowned at the postcard, as though straining to read a difficult passage.

I can't remember, she said finally, we sell so many of these.

I found this hard to credit but did not contradict her, I placed the postcard back in my suitcase.

Would *you* like to buy one, she asked.

I had not intended to, but as soon as she had put the question to me, the idea struck me with a certain force.

I returned to the rack and selected a postcard, not of the beach, but of the factory.

Setting it on the counter, I asked whether she knew what this building was, where in town I might find it, I would like to visit it while I was here, I said.

As she had with the previous postcard, she frowned at this one in silence, her eyes bright with what seemed to me a test-taker's anxiety, as though her brain had gone blank, foggy with the fear of producing a wrong answer.

Eventually she said, Oh, it's the hospital.

A hospital?

I studied the postcard again, and yes, it was true: the two structures that I had at first taken to be smokestacks were—I could see it now—in fact just slightly taller towers, composed of the same red brick as the main building, like separate wings flanking a general ward.

Though there were no ambulances or medical insignia visible, it was plain that the building was a hospital, I even wondered at myself for having mistaken it for a factory in the first place.

My understanding of the building shifted totally in that instant, I could no longer even see the towers as smokestacks, so clearly had their tower-being risen to the surface of the image, it was like watching a photograph develop in a chemical tray.

Yes, of course, I said, the hospital, do you know where it is?

She began to shake her head, but when she saw that I was still watching her expectantly, a worried expression crossed her face, and I could tell she felt a pressure to tell me something, anything, to summon some memory for my benefit.

That's right, she said, I remember now, it's just outside of town, about a mile.

Thanking her, I paid for the postcard and headed upstairs.

My room was next to 315, as I had hoped. Setting my suitcase down in the hall, I examined the door to 315.

No light was visible under the threshold, and a Do Not Disturb tag hung from the knob.

I knocked firmly, but inside nothing stirred.

Turning to my own room, I waved the white keycard over the reader, a bulky black box that whirred complexly before flashing a green light.

I had been prepared for this modern touch, but once inside I was surprised to find how much the room itself had been renovated, outfitted with the same contemporary amenities as any hotel: a flat-screen TV on the wall opposite the bed; an automatic coffee maker beside the coat closet in the vestibule; a charging hub on the nightstand, with ports for several devices.

The vintage façade belied this modern interior, which left an odd aftertaste of anachronism, as though the present had taken up residence in the shell of the past.

I called my client, who did not answer.

I left a voice message explaining that I had arrived at the motel and rented a room neighboring 315.

I would identify its occupant soon, I assured him, and send photos.

Against my bedroom's one window, there was a desk over-looking the parking lot and, beyond it, the beach.

I placed my client's photograph in the desk drawer, took a seat at the window.

My sedan was still the only car in the lot.

It was seeming more and more likely that the two of us—315 and I—were the sole guests in the building.

I tried to imagine who would rent a room here, at this vacant motel in this desolate town, and wait a week for my client to meet them.

They had signed the postcard with his wife's name, to convince him that he was receiving this message from a ghost, or from a memory.

But they had not signed her name, I corrected myself, only her initials, as though to preserve some privacy on this public correspondence: it was a signature that erased her identity as soon as it engraved it, the initials invited every other S.H. to occupy and overlay her name.

The subtext of the postcard was, Do you remember this place, I remember this place.

The letter writer remembered everything that his wife—in her final years—would have forgotten, and they were determined to make my client remember as well.

The message had arrived from beyond the end to return my client to the beginning.

A ghost, too, is a kind of memory disease.

The ghost has forgotten that it is dead, or the world has forgotten that it is gone, the ghost returns to reality the way that a mind returns to the past.

That appeared to be the only purpose of this poison-pen postcard campaign.

It was not a threat or blackmail, the letter writer was not making any demands or naming any ransom, they were merely reminding my client of a time in his life that, it seemed, he would prefer to forget.

But 315 had not written a *letter*, I corrected myself.

A postcard is not a letter, and they had chosen to send a postcard specifically, many things distinguish a postcard from a letter.

The lack of an envelope, the flatness, the photograph.

What distinguishes the postcard most of all, I thought, is the impossibility of response.

THE POSTCARD

The postcard arrives with no return address, from a destination that the sender has already left.

The message of every postcard, no matter what is written on it, is *I wish you were here*.

The sender calls out to an absent receiver from some present site, but by the time the postcard arrives, the sender will no longer be there, they will be absent themselves, the here will have become there in their memories, emptied of presence and become past.

As I write this, I wish it were the case that you were here, but also, *When you read this, I will be wishing that you had been there*.

The here always flickering between present and past, presence and absence.

Every postcard is the expression of this paradoxical desire.

Every one-way communication is, de facto, a postcard, every message to or from the dead: when my client visited his wife in the facility, he came to her as a postcard, the message *You are my wife* or *I am your husband* meant simply *I wish you were here*.

A ghost, too, is a kind of postcard.

315 had sent my client the postcard because they wished he was here, but he had disobeyed, had sent me here instead, I was the envoy he had dispatched in his place, his riposte, his postcard, whatever message they were planning to deliver to him would devolve to me.

As their initial invitation had devolved to me.

The devolution itself is what distinguishes the postcard: a postcard never has just one reader, after all; anyone can read what is written there, can become its addressee or its destination, every postcard is addressed to all possible yous.

These were the thoughts that I turned over in my mind, as I sat by the window.

As I kept vigil over the parking lot, waiting for 315 to return.

L ong after night had fallen the parking lot was still empty. I remained at the desk, watching headlights glide by the motel on the highway.

Occasionally a dark car slowed, as if about to pull in, but it always sped past in the end.

I began to wonder whether 315 could have been spooked by the sight of my car.

They would have been expecting my client to arrive, and they would be on the lookout for unfamiliar vehicles.

In any other motel, a motel with any other guests, this might not have been a concern, but here the presence of even a single car was conspicuous.

I remembered what the desk clerk had said, about a rear parking lot, and it occurred to me—several hours too late—that I should have moved my car out of sight.

I took my keys and headed downstairs.

On my way out of the building I noted the empty hallways, the abandoned front desk.

Truly there was no one else here.

In the parking lot I approached my car quietly, unlocking the door with the key rather than using the electronic fob, to avoid an errant beep.

But once I had slid into the driver's seat and placed the key in the ignition, a loud voice called out to me from inside the car.

You have arrived, the voice announced.

I startled, wheeling around to the empty back seat.

You have arrived, the voice repeated.

Smiling at my nerves, I reached up to the GPS device below the rearview mirror.

It was still on, I had forgotten to turn it off, it was finishing its script from earlier that day, from a drive that already felt like a week ago, it was stuck reciting these dead directions from the past.

I turned it off and pulled the car around back.

The rear lot was equally empty, and I made sure to park out of sight of the highway.

Back in my room, I tried to resume my vigil at the window, but the exhaustion from the flight and the drive had caught up with me.

Falling into bed, I entered without transition into a strange dream of a hospital.

When I woke the next morning, there were no new messages from my client.

Out the window, the front parking lot was still empty.

But when I checked the hallway, I saw that the Do Not Disturb tag had been removed from 315's door.

I tried knocking again, and no one answered.

Could they have left already?

It was possible they had come back in the night, after I had fallen asleep, and that they had left again early this morning, before I woke.

I hurried downstairs and found the front desk deserted as usual.

In the rear lot, mine was still the only car.

Maybe they had merely gone into town, I told myself, as I climbed into the driver's seat.

I would begin with the post office, I decided, it was possible that someone there would remember 315, or that 315 would be there themselves, monitoring a post-office box for my client's response.

I typed the address into the GPS and pulled out onto the highway.

Turn right, the cool robotic voice commanded.

In fifty feet, turn left.

It was another foggy day, I could not see five feet ahead of me, much less fifty.

The commands came minutes before I could see the intersections where I was supposed to carry them out.

I simply had to trust that there would eventually be a street to turn left onto.

I felt like a sleepwalker, a sleep-driver, blindly obeying an intelligence alien to my own.

I switched on my left turn signal, and sure enough, within seconds, a stop sign materialized out of the fog, out of the future.

Turning left, I soon found myself in what appeared to be downtown Ocean View, drifting down a main street of single-story shops.

A standard beach town, remarkable only for its mist and emptiness.

All the shop-windows were dark, the stores all closed.

There were no pedestrians on the sidewalks, and in the streets the parked cars had the distinct air of having been abandoned there.

I knew that it was the off-season, but even so the atmosphere of desertion unnerved me.

Moving block by block down the main street, I looked left and right for any signs of life.

Any of the parked cars could be 315's.

You have arrived, the voice announced.

And it was true, the post office had materialized on my left.

I pulled into the parking lot, but the building was dark as well, closed like everything else.

I coasted a slow circle in the empty lot, then entered the hospital's address into the GPS.

According to the map it lay directly ahead, a mile outside of town, just as the desk clerk had said.

But as I returned to the main street I could see no hospital in the distance, only a curtain of fog that never seemed to recede as I approached it.

Turn left, the GPS commanded eventually, and I switched on my blinker without thinking.

As I turned onto the next side street, I felt a physical twinge of lostness, like the tug of a compass needle in my chest, I knew at once that I was headed in the wrong direction.

But when I checked the GPS map the car's icon was still proceeding down the blue line of its designated route.

Turn left, the voice commanded again, and again I obeyed, switching on my blinker at the next stop sign.

I pulled onto another side street, a narrow alley lined with shabby condominiums: timeshares, I imagined, left vacant until summer, not a single person stood on the balconies.

With mounting disorientation I drove deeper into the fog.

Turn left, the GPS commanded again, for the third time.

I knew that this could not be correct—this was a residential neighborhood, I was being led farther and farther afield from the hospital—but I did not know why the GPS would keep sending me down this labyrinth of left turns.

Maybe there was a road closure, construction, maybe this was an elaborate detour.

Or maybe the GPS had encountered a glitch in its script.

Maybe it had become caught in a repetition, mechanically reiterating the same line.

Turn left, turn left, turn left.

Turning left at the next stop sign, I realized what must have happened.

The GPS must be guiding me back to the post office, I thought, sending me to my starting point.

I must have forgotten to update my destination in the address bar, and now I was trapped traveling in a loop.

Turn left, the voice commanded again, confirming my suspicions.

You have arrived.

I pulled to a stop and squinted through the foggy windshield.

But looming ahead of me, instead of the post office, was the unmistakable façade of the hospital: an immense brick building fronted by an iron gate.

Framed through the windshield, the hospital looked just as it had in the postcard, the entry gate was even centered in the same point in my field of vision.

It was as if I had come to a stop on the exact spot where the photographer had stood, occupying the vantage point or subject position of the camera.

The only difference now was the mist, which obscured everything except the two side towers, jutting just barely above the roof of fog.

As the fog drifted off, it seemed to pour forth from the towers in clouds, like smoke from smokestacks.

All the narrow windows in the building's façade were dark, apparently even the hospital was closed in this town.

Stepping out of the car, I approached the gate.

It was chained shut, with a heavy padlock on the chains, they had all begun to rust in the salt air, the hospital must have been shuttered for years.

Studying the façade, I pictured my client and S.H. inside, taking their tour of the factory.

I tried to imagine what my client would remember, if he were the one standing here now, with my eyes closed I summoned an image of myself with S.H., wandering the halls of the building before me: the iron machinery, the vast rooms, the droning of the docent.

When I returned to the car I entered the motel's address into the GPS again, reviewing the directions carefully before proceeding to the route.

Turn left, the voice commanded.

B oth parking lots were still empty when I arrived, and this time I did not bother parking out back.

315 must have checked out of the motel as soon as they had seen my car, they could be miles away by now, I would have to call my client and tell him that I had botched the case.

Inside the lobby, the same woman was stationed at the desk, sitting in the same position I had seen her in yesterday.

How may I help you, she asked.

I asked whether room 315 was available.

Ignoring my request, she smiled and asked whether I preferred smoking or nonsmoking.

I reminded her that I already had a room, 313, and as proof I flashed my white keycard, somewhat uselessly, there was no room number printed on it.

That's right, she said apologetically, I remember now, I'm sorry.

I would be happy to move to room 315, I told her, if it was available.

She closed her eyes, searching her memory.

I think someone is staying there, she said uncertainly.

I thanked her for her help and turned to leave.

But I hesitated at the desk, showing her my copy of the hospital postcard again.

I asked whether she knew anything about the hospital, or whether she had any brochures.

She studied the postcard and murmured, Hospital?

I had bought the postcard yesterday to send to my friend, I reminded her, and when I visited the hospital that morning it had appeared to be closed.

I don't know about that, she said, tapping the postcard, but this is the prison.

I studied the image again, more closely this time, and now that she had said it, yes, I could see it, leaning in I could make out minute but—once I had noticed them—unmistakable details that until that moment I had missed: the vertical bars in all the narrow windows; the glass glinting atop both towers, likely lookout stations for the guards; a thin vine of barbed wire looping around the gate.

Strange, I thought, how much it resembled the building I had visited today.

The main ward, the two towers.

I was certain it was a hospital that I had visited, for I had seen the word *hospital* on the GPS map.

But the two buildings were identical.

Perhaps the same building had, at separate times, served both functions: first it had been a prison and then it had become a hospital, a prison in the past and a hospital in the present, or vice versa, and perhaps now the city maintained a museum exhibit somewhere of all of the building's guises—factory, prison, hospital—with postcards showing historical photographs of its various façades.

I asked the woman whether one could visit the prison, and she smiled.

Oh yes, she said, it's just outside of town.

B ack upstairs, I saw that the Do Not Disturb tag had been restored to 315's doorknob.

I was surprised by the deepness of my relief.

They were still here, I had not lost them.

I knocked at their door, listening, but there was only silence.

Placing the prison postcard facedown against the wall, I wrote a message for them—*Ocean View, Room 313*—and signed it, I could not say why, with my client's initials.

I knelt to slide the card under their door, and as I was rising, something caught my eye.

Just below the handle of the doorknob was a keyhole.

In their transition from metal keys to plastic cards, the motel had installed the bulky black readers above the doorknobs, but they had not taken the additional step, it appeared, of removing the original keyholes.

I reached into my pocket and removed my client's key, the memento from his honeymoon.

With no expectation of success, I eased the key into the hole.

It still fit.

Checking the hall on either side, I gently rotated it until I heard the click of the latch.

The door swung open and I slipped inside, stepping around my postcard on the carpet.

Housekeeping, I called out in a false voice, and no one responded.

The room was empty.

It was, as I expected, laid out identically to my own.

The same coffee maker and coat closet in the vestibule, the same flat-screen TV opposite the bed, the same desk against the window.

A paper coffee cup sat on the desk, where the occupant of 315 must have been keeping their own vigil over the parking lot, waiting for my client to arrive, though the curtains were now closed.

I withdrew my phone and took a series of quick snapshots.

I opened the drawers of the nightstand, rifled through the wastebasket, looking for an ID or even a credit-card receipt, any piece of paper that would bear their name, but there was nothing, the room was bare of any trace except the paper cup.

Finally, opening the desk drawer, I found a copy of my client's photograph, the same image of him and S.H. posing beside the Ocean View road sign.

The sight of it there startled me at first, it didn't occur to me that 315 would have their own copy, for a moment I was gripped by a vision of them breaking into my room while I was gone, or while I slept, stealing the photo from my desk drawer.

I raised my phone and took a snapshot of the photo, maybe my client would know what to make of it, or who else would have a copy.

I walked to the window, tempted to draw the curtains.

If I drew them now, I knew, I ran the risk of being spotted.

Once 315 returned, they would have only to glance up at their window from the parking lot to see—by the parted curtains—that someone had trespassed into their room.

On the other hand, I reflected, if I left the curtains closed, I ran an even graver risk, for I would have no warning when they arrived.

They could be pulling into the parking lot at any moment—even now—without my knowledge.

After deliberating for what felt like minutes, I threw the curtains aside, and froze in place—with the reflexive paralysis of prey—when I saw a second car parked beside my own.

It was a black sedan indistinguishable from mine, it was clear—even from this distance—that it was the same make and model.

I lifted my phone to the window, quickly pinching the touch screen to zoom in on the license plate, and snapped a picture.

The car was empty, and the driver was nowhere to be seen in the lot; they must have already entered the building, must be making their way back to their room.

It was time to leave.

I hastily drew the curtains closed and started for the door, but I was not halfway across the room when I heard the whirring of the card reader, saw the knob turning.

Casting a panicked glance around me, I spotted the coat closet in the vestibule, its door ajar.

I ducked inside, easing the door shut just as the front door was opening.

The closet's door was louvered, and when the light switched on, the lamp's rays fell through the wooden slats in yellow lines, palely striping my hands.

I stepped back from the slats, withdrawing into the shadowed recesses of the clothes rack, and held my breath.

I readied the camera on my phone, prepared to snap a photo of 315 the moment that they passed into view before the slats.

As I waited, I tried to imagine their face, but I could picture only my client in his office, the young man in the photograph, S.H.

No one passed before the slats.

After the front door closed, there was a prolonged silence.

They seemed to be pausing at the threshold, as though surveying the room for disturbances.

What were they waiting for?

I cast my mind back, struggling to remember whether I had left any evidence, any traces of my presence there.

Then I heard a rustle like fabric against the carpet, and I formed a distinct mental image of someone kneeling to the floor.

The postcard.

Many moments passed, they must have been puzzling over the message I had left them—the message my client had left them, I corrected myself, I had signed it with his initials—until at last I heard the door open again and close behind them.

Through the thin plaster of the closet's back wall, the wall it shared with my own room's vestibule, I heard them knocking sharply at my door.

They knocked three times in succession, with increasing force, the hollow sound of it filled the closet, and as they waited in vain for me to answer, I waited in fear for them to return to their room.

They did not return.

Their footsteps softened down the hallway, followed by the sound of the stairwell's heavy metal door swinging shut.

They must be returning to the lobby, I realized, where they would attempt to interrogate the woman at the front desk about me.

Who bought this postcard, they would ask.

They would subject her to the same battery of questions that I had, I imagined, and her answers to them would prove just as useful.

Smoking or a nonsmoking, she would ask them.

Would *you* like to purchase a postcard?

Eventually they would reach the limits of their patience and leave, returning to their room.

I slipped free from the closet—leaving the door ajar as I had found it—and hurried back to my room, which I double-locked for good measure, drawing the chain across the bolt.

I went to the desk and checked the drawer: the photograph was still there, and nothing else had been disturbed.

It was only when I was sitting down, dialing my client, that I realized my error.

I had left the closet door ajar as *I* had found it.

But that was not how they had found it.

When they had stepped into the vestibule a moment ago, the closet door had been closed, because I had been hiding inside it.

Now, when they returned, they would see the door ajar.

Whether or not they registered this discrepancy, they would be able to detect that something in the room was off, that something had changed between their memory of the room and the room itself, and they would sense by this change that I had been there.

Moments later I heard them return.

No sooner had they entered their room than I heard the door slam shut again.

It had not taken them long to notice the closet, not long at all.

There came a harsh knock at my door.

There was no point hiding from them.

They had no proof that I was the one who had broken into their room, and even if they did, there was no danger now in answering the door.

After all, wasn't that what I had been sent here for?

To confront them and to confirm their identity, to determine—if I could—what they wanted from my client?

He was not paying me to hide from them and hold my breath.

And yet I felt a powerful reluctance to answer the door.

When I finally rose from the desk, I noticed a postcard being slipped across the threshold, I called out to them to wait but they did not answer.

I did not hear their footsteps pattering down the hall, or the clanging of the stairwell door, but by the stillness in the room— in the entire building, it seemed—I could tell that they were gone.

I picked up the postcard.

They had bought a copy of the same factory/hospital/prison, and on the back they had left a message.

Meet me at the facility, Room 315, S.H.

Facility?

This had been my client's term for S.H.'s final dwelling place, where he had left her to spend her last days alone.

Is this what 315 meant by facility?

Were they inviting me—or my client, I corrected myself—to leave Ocean View altogether, to meet them at the same facility where he had betrayed S.H. by abandoning her?

Or were they inviting him to meet them at the building on the postcard, which I had taken to thinking of as a factory/hospital/prison, but which they were now referring to as *the facility*?

A prison or a hospital could be described as a facility.

315 had never seen my face, I had been careful, they must assume that my client was the one staying in the room beside them.

As far as they knew, he had obeyed their postcard and followed them here, and now they wanted him to follow them further, back to the same building where he had taken his tour with S.H., all those years ago, this was the next step in their plan or their punishment for him.

This postcard was meant for him, not for me, the facility had nothing to do with me, its brick façade was addressed to him, to his memory, I wish you were here.

Only one thing troubled me, why were they still bothering to sign their postcards S.H.?

Truly they must want him to believe he was being haunted.

Because he had stopped visiting his wife in life, she would visit him in death, or make him visit her in death, this must be what they wanted him to believe.

I was growing tired of their game.

S.H. had no ghost, and even if she did, it would not return here, S.H. had forgotten Ocean View herself, in the end.

A ghost is the ongoingness of a memory, it stays behind on behalf of what it recalls, what it cannot forget, unfinished business, whereas a mind with no memory must produce no ghost, its business has been finished by forgetfulness.

Even if S.H.'s ghost had remained to haunt the facility, Ocean View would mean nothing to it, the name would not recall this town, this motel, their honeymoon, much less the room number 315, the words Ocean View would conjure only blankness in the ghost's eyes, its mind.

A ghost with gaps.

Even my client would mean nothing to it, it would not haunt him because it would not know him.

I am your husband, he would have to remind it, you are my wife.

It was likelier to haunt the wrong man, I thought, mistaking some stranger for its husband, than to recognize my client himself.

Returning to my desk, I looked out the window just in time to see 315's black sedan leaving the lot.

It turned onto the highway in the direction of Ocean View, and within seconds it was swallowed up by fog.

Opening my phone to the photo of their license plate, I ran the tag through a search and confirmed—I had suspected as much—that the car was a rental like my own, indeed that it was registered with the very same rental company, it probably came equipped with the same GPS device.

This was to be expected: the company operated the only rental booth at the only regional airport within a day's drive, anyone flying to N— would end up with a car from their fleet.

Still the coincidence disturbed me.

The fact that 315 and I had disembarked at the same airport, had rented the same car from the same company, had been guided through the fog by the same voice, had been sitting room by room in the same motel, with the same photograph in the same desk drawer, seemed meaningful.

I sent the snapshots of 315's room, the photograph, and the latest postcard to my client, and asked whether he knew what to make of them.

He did not respond.

There was nothing left to do but follow after them.

I took my time gathering my things.

There was no rush, I reasoned.

If they wished my client was there, they would be waiting.

T urn left, the voice commanded.

There were still no other cars on the road.

The fog was thicker than ever, through the gaps that appeared in my windshield I barely recognized the highway, the beach, I was totally reliant on this voice.

I tried calling my client again, but his phone went to voicemail.

I began to leave a message updating him on the investigation, but midway through my explanation, I trailed off.

Why was I leaving a message in the first place?

Turn left, the voice commanded.

Why had my client not answered the phone, or called me back, or responded to my messages—even once—since I had arrived in Ocean View?

Many explanations occurred to me.

Maybe he had disappeared.

Maybe he had hired me only to create a diversion, or an alibi.

Perhaps he had been the one to mail himself the postcard to begin with, for all I knew he could be the one staying in 315.

Or maybe he really did believe that S.H. was haunting him, and he had sent me here as a decoy, a substitute husband for her to haunt instead.

If she could not remember him anyway, he must have thought, then why should he be the one to return to her, any other man could step just as well into his name, his place, his fate, why not send a stranger, why not me.

Turn left, the voice repeated.

Yellow lines flashed out of the fog.

The farther I drove from the motel, the more distant a concern my client became.

He would never answer or call me back, I knew.

I had no expectation of seeing him again, which meant that the case was my own now, if I persisted in following 315 it could be only for my own reasons.

Turn left.

I was the one who wanted to know their identity, not my client, I was the one who their postcards—in a manner of speaking—had been addressed to.

I was their postcards' destination, the one who was destined to return, drawn to the here toward which they wished me.

It was not too late to turn back, I thought.

The fog pressed against my car from all sides.

You could drive to N—, I told myself, to the airport, and leave Ocean View behind.

You have arrived, the voice announced.

Obeying, I slowed, and the brick building loomed above the fog looming before me.

The front gate was open now, and in the lot a single car— 315's black sedan, the double of my own—was parked near the entrance.

The building still resembled a hospital—on the GPS map it was still marked *hospital*—but staring at it I could not shake the faint penitentiary afterimage that overlaid it.

The building itself looked just as abandoned as before, all the windows dark, and while I could not see I could well imagine the bars in the windows.

I parked beside 315's car.

You don't have to go inside, I thought, as I exited my car and approached the building.

You can still turn back, I told myself, as I tested the front door.

It was unlocked, swinging open when I pushed, and I realized that I was wrong, there was no turning back now.

Indeed, as I stepped over the threshold, I understood that this was only a false threshold, I must have crossed the true threshold long before: even on the day I had driven into Ocean View there had been no turning back, every yellow highway line had flashed the fresh threshold of my trespass.

Inside the building, the lobby was dusty and dim: a desk, a floor of institutional linoleum, a barren wire rack where brochures might once have been, or postcards.

There were two stairwells to choose between, a door on my right and a door on my left, each leading to one of the towers that flanked the main building.

There were no indications that 315 had gone through one or the other, I had no way of deciding between them.

Just as I was about to turn right, a loud voice called out in the lobby, a disembodied robotic voice, resounding in the space as if from a hidden speaker.

Turn left, the voice commanded.

I scanned the ceilings for the source of the voice, but there was nothing to be seen.

Turn left, the voice commanded again.

I obeyed, heading up the lefthand stairwell.

On the third floor I proceeded down a long and narrow hallway.

The doors to either side of me—306, 313—were all closed, their thresholds dark.

At 315 I saw a sliver of yellow light pouring out from beneath the sill.

I tried the knob, but it was locked, and when I knocked, no one answered.

I almost turned to leave, but then I thought to withdraw the Ocean View motel key from my pocket.

315, the diamond tag read.

It fit perfectly in the lock.

I turned the key to the left, until I heard the click of the latch.

I've got you, I thought as I opened the door, expecting to find—I was surprised by the clarity of the intuition—my client.

But inside the room there was an older woman, the same age as he, the same age as the desk clerk, and the same age too—it occurred to me—as S.H. would have been, if she had lived.

She stood before a clean white cot.

I had been prepared to come face-to-face with 315 in this room, whoever 315 was, but despite all the possible faces I had assigned them, I could tell that this woman was not who I was looking for, she was not the person I had followed here.

She was wearing a green uniform, halfway between a nurse's scrubs and a janitor's jumpsuit, she must be one of the keepers of this place, the custodian or the docent of whatever facility this was.

Against the wall there was a wooden wardrobe with louvered doors, for a moment I was gripped by a vision of 315 hiding inside, spying on us through the slats.

I stepped forward and the door swung shut behind me, clicking.

Who are you, the woman asked, what are you doing here.

I introduced myself, and she brightened.

My husband had that name, she told me.

I chose to ignore this, I could tell by her tone—her tense—that her husband was dead, I did not want to ask about him.

I explained that I was looking for someone, I had followed them here, and then I asked, eyeing the wardrobe, whether she had seen anyone besides me.

Turn left, the voice announced, so loud I jumped.

Vainly I searched the ceiling again, from corner to corner, but there were no speakers anywhere.

Where is he, I asked the woman, who did not appear to have heard the voice.

She nodded politely, as though she had not understood the question.

I turned to leave, but the door had locked automatically, there was no keyhole within the room.

I struggled with the knob for a minute before pounding on the door in frustration, three times in succession.

Hello, I called, addressing I don't know who, the hallway was empty, hello, let me out.

I tried calling out that I was not my client, they had the wrong man, it was a misunderstanding, if they unlocked the door I would leave and never return.

The silence throughout the building was utter.

Who are you, the woman asked again from behind, in the same tone, as though I had just walked through the door.

Again I introduced myself, again she brightened.

My husband had that name, she repeated, and she pronounced my name.

I flinched to hear her say it, I could feel the walls of my own name weakening.

I walked to the woman's window and drew the curtain, she had a clear view of the facility's parking lot.

315's car was gone, it had vanished from beside my own, mine was now the only vehicle visible anywhere, I was alone here.

The destination is on your left, the voice announced, but to my left there was nothing but the cot.

Suddenly overcome by exhaustion, I sat down on the stiff mattress, just to catch my breath, I told myself.

I needed to gather my strength, break down the door.

315 could not have gotten far.

You look like someone I know, the woman told me.

Then she exclaimed, I know who it is, you look just like my husband.

I smiled weakly.

Oh, she sighed, I wish he were here, he's going to take me home.

Don't you like it here, I asked.

No, I'm leaving any day now, I've already packed my bags.

She walked toward the wardrobe, and I braced myself.

But when she opened the louvered doors there were only several overstuffed suitcases inside, the same suitcases, I suspected, that she had been brought here with, what was this place.

You see, she said, I'll be ready when he comes, ready when my husband comes to take me home.

I thought of my client's photograph, their car loaded with suitcases for their honeymoon.

It's me, I told her, I am your husband, you are my wife, I'm here to take you away.

She studied my face warily, but the suspicion lasted only a second, recognition overcame her.

She clasped her hands to her chest and embraced me with thin arms, I held her frailty against me, felt a sudden dampness on my shoulder.

Oh it is you, it's really you, you came.

We're going back to Ocean View, I promised her, stroking her brittle hair, to that little motel where we stayed, the very same room, room 315, do you remember, I've booked it already.

She sighed at the memory and I let her go.

By the light in her eyes I could tell she was picturing, if not the Ocean View itself, then a generic hotel, the received image of two lovers alone together in a sunny room, white bedsheets, white beach, something she had seen in movies or in dreams.

Is it true, she asked me, are we really going?

Yes, I said, but first—

Her face darkened, the hotel was already shifting bitterly, in her mind, back into the prison or hospital or factory in which she was trapped.

But first, I said, I need you to tell me, it's very important, did anyone else visit today?

No, she answered, no one ever visits me here, no one even calls, you're the first person to come in all this time, can you believe it?

I believe it, I said, but I could have sworn I saw—

Let me think, she said, closing her eyes.

I closed my own eyes, just to rest them, I told myself, just for a moment.

With my eyes closed, in the darkness and the silence, the voice resounded somehow even more loudly in my skull, I could not tell whether it was before me or behind me.

The destination is on your left, the voice reassured me.

Oh, we're going, the woman announced excitedly, like the bride that, somewhere inside her, she still was.

Then she laughed at herself and asked, Wait, where are we going?

Who are you?

And now I truly was tired, now I could not have opened my eyes if I had wanted to.

I heard myself pronounce my client's name.

My husband had that name.

I wish you were here.

You have arrived.

MEDUSA

AT THE ITALIAN HISTORICAL INSTITUTE FOR THE
Middle Ages, in the Library of the House of Literature in Rome,
an apotropaic mosaic Medusa gazes up from the hallway floor.
She protects the library by warding off evil influences, turning
them to stone. Several poets in the library's collection have fantasized about turning to stone, or turning their beloved to stone.
Visitors may read these poems under the aegis of the gorgo-
neion. *I have built a monument more lasting than bronze / and set
higher than the pyramids of kings*, Horace writes in Ode 3.30. *Not
marble nor the gilded monuments / Of princes shall outlive this
powerful rhyme*, Shakespeare writes in Sonnet 55, *But you shall
shine more bright in these contents / Than unswept stone*. The
classical project of literature is to defeat death by fashioning a
superior statue. Books are just sculptures that don't erode: they
extend mortal forms across immortal time, preserving imperma-
nent pasts for an infinite future. Yesterday survives as a pebble
in tomorrow's boot. Medusa may be viewed as the patron saint
of this immortality project. Like a poet, she regards people from
the point of view of petrifaction. To see her is to be statuefied,
eternalized. That is why a gorgon guards the archive. Within this
library, whose manuscripts have survived for centuries, she sur-
veys all visitors with tesserae eyes. Everything here, she seems
to say, will endure like stone. That is the promise the Medusa
makes: has been making, decade after decade, with her undecay-
ing mosaic face. The evil she is warding off is time.

ACKNOWLEDGMENTS

My thanks to the following institutions for their generosity and hospitality: the Berlin Writers' Workshop, especially Carleen Coulter, Ben Mauk, Anne Posten, and Ryan Ruby; the Historic Phillips House, especially Robin Christianson and Kim Miller; the Iowa Writers' Workshop, especially Connie Brothers, Sam Chang, Sasha Khmelnik, Deb West, and Jan Zenisek; the University of Iowa English Department, especially Kaveh Akbar, Lori Branch, Corey Campbell, Elizabeth Rodriguez Fielder, Ed Folsom, Claire Fox, Loren Glass, Louisa Hall, Donika Kelly, Brooks Landon, Kathy Lavezzo, Paige Lewis, Christopher Merrill, Barb Pooley, William Rhodes, Hannah Sorrell, Harry Stecopoulos, Garrett Stewart, Kate Torno, Jonathan Wilcox, and Shannon Yost; the University of Iowa Nonfiction Writing Program, especially John D'Agata, Melissa Febos, and Cherie Hansen-Rieskamp; the *Kenyon Review* Writers Workshop, especially Elizabeth Dark; and Warren Wilson College's MFA Program for Writers, especially Debra Allbery. Thank you to Tim Conroy for helping me find a space to write in Iowa City.

This book was written with the support of an Old Gold Fellowship at the University of Iowa. Thank you to the College of Liberal Arts and Sciences, especially Deans Roland Racevskis and Sara Sanders.

Grazie mille to the American Academy in Rome, where many of these stories were written, as well as to everyone in the community: the administration, staff, and chefs; my fellow fellows and their fellow travelers; and the visiting scholars, affiliated artists, and members of the literature board. Particular thanks to Gianpaolo Battaglia, Michael Beaman, Anne Carney, Tom Carpenter, Jim Carter, Judy Chung, Lydia Conklin, Steve DiBenedetto, Anthony Doerr, Sofia Ekman, Allison Emmerson, Nate Emmerson, James Galvin, Allan Gurganus, Tiziana del Grosso, Scott Harlow, Sebastian Hierl, Edward Hirsch, Zaneta Hong, T. Geronimo Johnson, John Kamitsuka, Camille Kondratieff, Eric Kondratieff, Lynne Lancaster, Nicolás Leong, Mark Letteney, Alessandro Lima, Michelle Lou, Howard Michels, Shawn Miller, Vicky Moses, John Ochsendorf, Kyle Pierce, Austin Powell, Francine Prose, Kirstin Valdez Quade, Mark Robbins, Michael Saltarella, Victoria Steele, Gabriel Soare, Virginia Virilli, and Lauren Watel.

Thank you to the following readers for their insight and support: Jin Auh, Kyle Edgerton, Greg Gerke, Elliott Holt, Evan James, Gerald Maa, Carmen Maria Machado, Ben Mauk, Lincoln Michel, Bradford Morrow, Nadxieli Nieto, Lynne Nugent, Eric Obenauf, Sam Risak, Benjamin Samuel, Abram Scharf, Pat Sims, Tony Tulathimutte, and Eliza Wood-Obenauf. Special thanks to Sam Chang. Melted olives for Liz McTernan.

'La "mummia di Grottarossa"' and 'Medusa' were written in dialogue with the photographer Sze Tsung Nicolás Leong, as part of a collaborative project that he and Judy Chung initiated at the American Academy in Rome. The stories were originally exhibited alongside Nicolás's photographs at the American Academy in Rome and the House of Literature in Rome, respectively. Thanks to Nicolás for permission and assistance in reproducing his images, as well as to the House of Literature in Rome; the Istituto Storico Italiano per il Medioevo, Rome; and the Ministry of Culture – National Roman Museum, Palazzo Massimo.

'Pecking Order' draws language and concepts from Peter Godfrey-Smith's *Other Minds* and Temple Grandin's *Animals Make Us Human.*

'Portonaccio Sarcophagus' draws language and concepts from Janet Huskinson's "'Unfinished Portrait Heads" On Later Roman Sarcophagi: Some New Perspectives.' The Nietzsche passage is from a letter to Jacob Burckhardt and was first encountered in Jalal Toufic's *(Vampires): An Uneasy Essay on the Undead in Film.* The full Levinas quotation is 'I cannot say at what moment you have the right to be called "face"… I don't know if a snake has a face,' and was first encountered in Jacques Derrida's *The Animal That Therefore I Am.*

'Medusa' draws language and concepts from Michael Clune's *Writing Against Time* and Aaron Kunin's 'Shakespeare's Preservation Fantasy.'

ILLUSTRATION CREDITS

4: Sze Tsung Nicolás Leong: *1887, 1981: Palazzo Massimo, Roma* (2019) (courtesy of the artist; by permission of the Ministry of culture – National Roman Museum, Palazzo Massimo)

71, 73: Jean-Pol GRANDMONT: *Sarcophage de Portonaccio— Palazzo Museo Massimo* (Wikimedia, Creative Commons, 2011)

79, 81: Courtesy of the author

202: Sze Tsung Nicolás Leong: *1650: Istituto Storico Italiano per il Medioevo, Oratorio dei Filippini, Roma* (2019) (courtesy of the artist; by permission of the Istituto Storico Italiano per il Medioevo, Rome)